Ut

Utopia

Peter Cowlam

_____cHp_____
CentreHouse Press

British Library Cataloguing in Publication Data
A catalogue record for this book is available from the
British Library

ISBN 978-1-902086-25-5

In remembrance of Holly Cowlam, an innocent in these events, but who well knew the Street of the Musicians.

Utopia

Utopia

1

No one knew much about Zora Murillo, or the source of her zillions (an exaggeration surely), on her sudden arrival in Hoe. Almost the first thing she did was sink unfathomable sums into the Pleiades, a majestic, crumbling ruin at the hub of our town. Its twenty-five rooms were faded through neglect, where no one other than travellers – down at heel, and down on their luck – ever stayed for long, except by mistake. The bar downstairs still ran, from late afternoon till dinner, with a clientele of builders, mechanics, a cobbler, a freelance sign writer, two competing window cleaners, and a flaky-haired painter and decorator.

The bar was the first thing Zora ripped out, though she kept the builders on to do the work, who brought to the hotel's cobbled frontage a fleet of yellow skips. Filling them daily were cheap timbers in an old, once fashionable reddish stain, the rotten plaster hacked from the walls and ceilings, and the country-woven carpeting, whose reds, jets and golds were discoloured by decades of beer spills. She did not have to evict the squatters upstairs. They left of their own accord, with the noise and upheaval, and what had been home reduced to a shell. Its eviscerate state was final and at its nadir once the old wiring and lead pipes were piled with the rest of the debris into those skips.

The work got fanfares in the local press, and headlines three weeks running. Someone discovered that Zora had also bought the Faun Hotel twenty miles away in Yo, a lot different from the Pleiades. *That* was in a good state of repair, though had calcified into English rural pleasantries fifty years out of date. The waitresses were pinafored, and there was a resident chef, whose background was minor public school. The foyer had low leather settees and shag-pile carpets. It was dark with oak panelling, and was adorned on its table tops with country magazines. It told a stolid sort of time by a longcase clock, and had a stag's head and puffed-up portraits hanging on the walls. The car parking was extensive, adjacent to a stream with ornamental bridge. Patrons drove Land Rovers and wore tweeds, and came for the fish dinners and the homity pie on its lunchtime menus. Zora had no intention of changing the Faun's ethos, but for the Pleiades she had different ideas, as we shall see.

2

The *Valley Tribune* is tucked away in a ramshackle glass and timber building, a five-minute walk from the Pleiades, in Tinclian Mews, a location famed for its cheese shop. Andrew Mawdrie, his wardrobe a blare of cravats and yachting blazers, was its senior reporter. He was summoned on a bleak afternoon – the sky ponderous with snow – and with purpose strode to the hotel, and round to its cobbled walk at the rear, and a car park pocked in its macadam, and littered with empty oil drums. Zora, in deep furs and a head scarf knotted under her chin, met him there, Mawdrie alert and ready with his notebook. She led him into the ruins of the garage, where he looked forward to a scoop, or good copy at least. Both looked round. The walls were damp, and the aura cavern-like, a latter-day Lascaux, careless with its graffiti. She was glad he had come, now that Mawdrie cited his credentials, explaining that journalism wasn't his limit. He'd got a reputation as a local historian, and had extensive knowledge of the Hoe Valley and its prominent personalities, past and present. He had written articles and given talks, and had even edited books. Zora looked at him and must have remained inscrutable. She told him she'd got plans, but left it at that. Mawdrie, tantalised, pressed, but couldn't discover what those plans were. Then finally she thrust both hands into her furs and shrugged, daring him to keep the conversation going.

Well, if that was it. Originally, he said, the garage had been a stable, with a hayloft above. That bit was dismantled when the Pleiades was turned into a private house, its owner a man with a single-barrelled name, but 168th in line for the throne. The stable metamorphosed into a garage when there were just four cars in the whole of Hoe, and was home to an Alvis 12/40 open two-seater, its livery a metallic blue, and well looked after by a boy who shone the chrome and coachwork. There were wars, stock-market crashes, a flaw in civilisation generally. Then came the renewed scourge of industrial unrest, in a new world where everyone had cars. By that time that distant heir had sold up and left for the one weather-tight room in the decay of his family pile, where his daughter-in-law ran a stall selling honey. The Pleiades reverted to its earlier iteration, but as a hotel rather than a roadhouse, when the garage filled with lumber. It didn't fare well, and was popular only with commercial travellers, selling feeds and farm machinery – grey, threadbare-looking men in a losing contest with the ravages of English recessions, one piled on another. The garage bit was rented out to a lone mechanic, who fled when the hotel sank into deeper failures and its guests were replaced by squatters, who'd studied the paperwork and knew their rights. Since then, said Mawdrie, the place has hosted raves, was a crack house, was the scene of torture when turf wars upcountry had to be settled, that chain you see hanging there the last remnant of its strappado. Zora shivered. 'All well and good,' she said. What she wanted to know was could he recommend a decent builder?

3

The article Mawdrie put out juxtaposed the glamorous Zora Murillo with the filth and squalor he had reported on over past decades, all of it emanating from the Pleiades. There were drug busts, money laundering, lock-ins, with the back rooms and garaging a focus for gang wars county-wide. He thought he paid her a compliment when this chic new addition to an enlightened little market town he likened to an Egyptian queen biblical in her ancestry. In reality he probed for the source of her wealth, in musing she might have been heiress to one of those industrial magnates who, in centuries past, had opened up the West, or a Hollywood goddess retracing her English lineage. He would live to regret that blunder. Zora read his article, and was toxic with rage, and with a 5,000-word essay penned her reply. It had the essence of scripture, and no lack of authority, adding up to a point-by-point refutation of the Mawdrie slur, as she called it, a ragbag of small-town thinking. She wondered by what order of posterity she was linked to the *femme fatale* of pre-Christian Roman politics, or a pampered scion of the robber barons big in steel or rail, or a manipulated starlet. If it was down to direct historical analogy, she'd point him to the daughter of Michael Psellus, in whose *Chronographia* is chronicled Byzantium's awesome military power degenerating into an effete bureaucracy, a fate suffered by all flagging empires, as applicable to news and media as it was to imperial statecraft.

Mawdrie went and looked it up. With no real strategy other than to humour her, he launched out on a lecture for his readers with the story of Psellus's daughter, Styliane, though in what context he wasn't clear. At age nine Styliane was tall, elegant, graceful in her movements, modest in her clothing, a girl admired by the rich and powerful, in whose company she behaved with artless perfection – no tricks, no boasting, all done without cosmetics. But she fell ill, with a plague-like disease, whose mark was fever and eruptions, and the ruination of her looks. She lay for twenty days with the pain of her sores. When those on her face improved her parents hoped for full recovery. But the fever worsened, and she'd no reserves of strength to resist the onslaught. She couldn't speak or eat. On the thirty-first day she raised her hands in a gesture of farewell, and after that the house was filled with mourners. At her funeral she was unrecognisable from that unspoilt beauty she had been, covered as she was in sores. You can imagine Psellus and his wife, and their lament, and a grief they didn't recover from. How this might have been paralleled in Zora's own life was left to someone other than Mawdrie to tell us, with access to a different order of information. But we'll come to that.

4

The main drag in Mawdrie's tiny historic town is a hill, snaking west on its ascent. It is East Street at its foot, which the Pleiades dominates. It narrows into the Borné halfway to the summit – there are fashion and charity shops, and a restaurant – and it grades into the High Street uppermost, a grey empyrean boasting a sub-Post Office, a junk shop and an ironmonger. The Borné was scene of a recent precedent to Zora's great experiment in Hoe, with Louella Ångström – another blow-in – who revamped the Happy Parakeet, a glass and aluminium-fronted place on the bend with East Street. When Louella, or Lou as she's called, took over the Parakeet, it was a coffee-shop-cum-eatery, with events pencilled in for weekday evenings. It had rough deal tables and a weary-looking menu. The highlight was Wednesday night, or curry night, with the closed sign hung up promptly at eight p.m. Its moment of flamboyance was a late Saturday lunch for Hoe's MP, who got his surgery duties out of the way and breezed in wearing country tweeds and sounding like a stentor. He wanted, and could never get, a window seat. That was not his only tragedy. He had lost family and others in the last world conflagration, and did his bit for racial harmony heading up immigration committees. He led the debates in the Commons. I personally testify that Wednesday nights were a masterpiece of blandness, a miasma of chickpea and aubergine dishes, indifferent even to the unadventurous, and accompanied by a no-hoper strumming a guitar and singing slushy songs.

Lou swept all that dubious charm aside, with a change of chef, the menu and décor, and for fanfare inspired a column by Mawdrie himself, writing in his *Valley Tribune*. He sampled, gratis, having tucked in an ostentatious serviette, one of the Parakeet's rare blue steaks, served up on an artistic-looking platter, courtesy Diggory, the main man in the kitchen. She annulled the entertainment contracts, and used her reputation gained previously in the parched groves of academe, engineering a warm welcome up at Stoneleigh, that place isolated on the moor. Mawdrie soon found out that Louella was tacitly acknowledged as having ghosted Horace Freelan's memoirs once he'd retired from office (the cabinet, the Blair era), a project got to grips with once he had taken up his new post as Vice-

Chancellor of the Tron Partick Institute. The TPI was a stallion of research and invention located on the southeast coast. Lou, until *she'd* retired, had been a senior in the TPI's Faculty of Arts and Humanities, and for the last twenty years had headed up its Harald Fritzsch Building, a notable design by architects Henning Larsen (the kind of stuff Mawdrie always found impressive). What Mawdrie didn't know, and I was not about to tell him, was what had precipitated *Lou's* retirement. Painfully, that was the collapse of her midlife love affair with a man called Anatole, provenance unknown. Anatole had been seduced by one Bez D'Soon, a female poet doing her MA (Contemporary Urban Narrative) at the Tron Partick. Pointedly, Bez had been careful in leaving plentiful clues as to her liaison almost everywhere Lou was likely to discover them – on her blog, on her Facebook page, all over YouTube. More on that maybe.

For the moment it's Stoneleigh. That institution takes its name from the eighteenth-century house on the moorland estate in whose grounds the conservatoire is. I go there often. Lou probably knew all in its upper echelon, and the best of its teaching staff. It's a recorded fact she called on Gavin Sord, who lived in the Street of the Musicians, a five-minute walk from the Happy Parakeet. Sord's connections with Stoneleigh pre-date his concert career, a life ceaselessly on the road, now at its end, as today he spends his time in composition. His catalogue lists mostly pithy modernist pieces, a dedicated oeuvre Mawdrie doesn't understand (there are no tunes, he says) and one that never rates a mention in the arts pages of the *Valley Tribune*. Hoe is not aware of its talents.

Lou invited him over to the Parakeet one morning, and asked him to put its piano through its paces – a sad-looking upright with brass fitments and a jangling, twangling tone. Gavin tried it with scales, then a few chords lifted from Scarlatti, then Scriabin – and was withering. Said Lou, it was not hard to detect the finality (it has remained absolute) in the way he closed the lid on that ill-fated instrument. 'I cannot play this,' he said. Louella understood what it was to be an aesthete, something I saw first-hand, when I bumped into her up at Stoneleigh. The summers were a spell of night concerts put on by its students, who between them had the whole repertoire – plain chant, Baroque, the axis Mozart-Haydn, the full force of Romantic orchestration, the modern arc Stravinsky to John Adams. We met for coffee in the intervals, and if the weather had changed, unseen by us – for the moor brought fog, rain, wind – I'd offer her a lift home (a detour I did not mind). It was a short walk to where she lived – a severe, Gothic-looking little palace, which I always park outside but never enter. Anyway, the point is she placed an ad on the Stoneleigh notice boards, wanting singers, string, wind, brass and percussion-players down at the Parakeet. Soon she'd got resident trios, quartets, quintets, and an ambitious programme that ranged from Bach to Bartók.

5

But really it's about Zora. She could not fail to notice on her entry into Hoe the lavish spectacle the Parakeet got in the pages of the *Tribune*. Mawdrie loved the menus, and shovelled his way through Diggory's totality of pastas and *ragout*. Refined in his degustation, an ear half-cocked to Schubert, or puzzling on the last quartets of Villa-Lobos, he settled on the *vermicelli* as his regular main. I personally can vouch for the *rigatoni* tubes. Zora looked on indignantly, and pledged to make the Pleiades the social hub of the valley's quaintly famous town. She turned attention to its main bar, in its lack of professional appeal. Then came the rooms, converted *en suite* every one, and spotlessly appointed. She enlarged the parking. That required the revised orientation of its bays, whose layout was inefficient, and turning the stable-workshop-garage, or latterly house of torture, into a covered lot for her wealthier clientele. A flat roof off a balcony, whose vista was the delivery yard, she enclosed in a glass balustrade and turned into a terrace, with seating and parasols, which proved popular at cocktail time. Her flunkeys she liveried in white shirts and black waistcoats, and gave everyone a name badge – including her Polish interns, all with impossible surnames. The Pleiades' frontage was given street seating and outdoor heaters, where she snared the last of the town's tobacco lobby, in its brotherhood of smokers – a facility the Parakeet couldn't match.

But what to do with the ballroom, abandoned as a hopeless last vestige of opulence, in Zora's mind the image of sunken remains, a lost *Lusitania* in a landlubber world. She smartened it up. Replaced the lighting rigs. Got it re-floored. She made sanitary its back-stage facilities, and hung up a glitter ball. She asked, what popular acts had Hoe already got? Well, there was a stand-up poet, big on empathy. There was a fire-eater. There was a red-headed juggler, and a happy-faced retiree who played the hurdy-gurdy. 'That,' Zora said, 'is greatly disappointing,' and told Andrew to scour his archives for anything more inspiring. What he came up with was no better, according to her, the best being a jazzman who'd made a name in local radio.

Said Zora, 'You call this the UK's funkiest town?'

Mawdrie defended himself. 'Why yes. We have a currency.' One pound sterling equals one pound Hoe. Ho ho.

I had known Zora's impatience. Confronted by Mawdrie's granite, masculine imagination, boyish without wonderment, she threw up her hands and found her alternative somewhere front of house, where she and Izabela Dziubińska, her manager ('we cannot call her manageress'), went at it heart-to-heart. A compliant, energetic Izabela assured her there was little she'd overlook, as she delved as deep into the nation as Google allowed, beginning her search for less depressing stuff.

'Any luck there?' I asked. We'll see.

6

I have a compact riverside property for the few days I am here, a loggish-looking place with shallow roof, glass doors to the patio, a long incline turfed and paved to the jetty. The buoys bob. Leashed, and secured with the best of my Scout knots – for yes, I learned them all – is the little launch I use, and lend to other users, with trips up and down the Dwar. Some put in for picnics in a glade, sunny days only, summer and autumn. Zora, less keen on that, prefers walking, as far along the river as its path allows. That, on parting its parallel line, loops up and around into woods, brakes, brambles and farmland, and plunges down finally to the Huntsman's Arms. You get a good lunch, served outside in a maze of clematis, or indoors in a long, rectangular, wood-dark dining room, with antique furnishings, big heavy chairs and tables – all deeply scarred – and an enormous canopied fireplace. There are grasses in a jeroboam. She called on me one misty morning, and lounged in the hall while I laced my boots and adjusted the neckwear I had got for Christmas, then led the way across the footbridge, its ribs frosted, its framework a reflected blur in the water, still and grey and tranquil. The morning was placid, church bells receding. I did not initiate our conversation, any of it, and before we had got to the Huntsman I knew what was on her mind, which at that time was mostly Mawdrie, who meant well but said the wrong things. I kept urging her to friendly overtures towards Louella Ångström, to whose Parakeet Mawdrie had given his five-star rating.

What could be done? Zora's stand-off, she said, was nothing personal. The reality was, family political breeding, and the acumen it had given her, only intensified

Louella's presence as a rival. Good relations were useful, but friendship was out of the question.

'You sound very sure,' I said, as I didn't think it followed necessarily, though I knew the worst of what she'd seen. I got no reply and humoured her up to a point, telling her it did no harm to keep on terms with Mawdrie – for his column inches, if that meant anything. I had my doubts.

'What are you suggesting?'

I said before opening up the ballroom, and the Pleiades generally, and before that national influx of clowns and acrobats, what about an official opening? Why not regale Hoe and its quilted country property-owners with cocktails and canapés? 'You could have cabaret, champagne, scissors, a ribbon. Mawdrie likes to write that stuff.'

She'd give it some thought, though had only just paid off her architect-cum-builder, with the painters and decorators last to leave. There was still a smell of newness, pungent. Also she couldn't speak for Izabela, as so far no names had gone into the database.

'Oh but give it time,' I said.

She needed a lot. Still no decision was made when I next passed the Parakeet, where Diggory was testing out his latest specials, devilled sprats and roasted half-shell scallops. Mawdrie was at his table with his bib tucked in, with a house Greek salad on the side. Lou, who had still got her scarf and coat on, must have just come in from somewhere, and was talking animatedly with him.

I thought better of going in.

7

The grand opening. The canapés were served by middle-aged men and lithe young women suited in white top hat and tails. Their zigzags across the floor were a practised art, an above-the-shoulder vertigo, with only a feigned potential for mishap in the angles they tipped their salvers through. The piano was also white. I heard its player had a flight booked for New Orleans, and for his detour in and out of Hoe stuck to a repertoire of elevator tunes. Volume-wise, it didn't rise above a heartbeat, as had been his strict instruction.

Zora insisted my entrance was with Louella – 'You'll have Louella on your arm' – a formality I agreed to without querying the motive, and Lou smiled at quirkily. She drove in from the moor, in *faux* furs and silky shoes, and ushered me into the office upstairs at the Parakeet. She'd got some last-minute paperwork, and was on the phone – heated at times. We strolled out and round the bend of the Borné and into East Street. It was breezy, an east wind whipping up, a dampish cold by the time we'd got to the Pleiades. Izabela smiled broadly and hung Louella's coat, and showed us the stairs to the gallery above, all of it newly carpeted. We went up, softly, and to a soft landing, and were met at the double doors of the ballroom. It was one of Zora's bellhops, got up ludicrously in a coat, waistcoat and breeches – old new Europe reimagined, Zora's idea of society Baroque. The bellhop bowed and opened the doors, where instantly I knew everyone gathered, as did

Louella, who went off and mingled, and sipped at a
pineapple juice.

The thing went off well, a success, though it miffed
Andrew that Zora hadn't chosen him as Louella's escort, as
I found out close to midnight, when with his jacket off and
his sleeves rolled up he was sulking at the bar. I bought him
another drink. He asked how it was I knew everyone in
Hoe – and so friendly with Lou – as after all I'd only odd
days here. I reminded him: I worked as gossip columnist at
the *Bluffington*, whose reach from behind its paywall
meant I had got to know everyone, literally. He raised a
glass meekly and said he'd never shelled out to get there, so
didn't know exactly what it was I wrote, and about whom.

'What things *do* you write?'

I hedged, and told him my specialism was out-of-the-
way stuff. He pressed and I had to give examples. Once, I
said, when passing through New York, I cornered Martin
Amis, having pinned him down for interview, subject
matter exile, the writers Saul Bellow and VN, and the
international role of butterfly socialites. But his cell phone
went off and the thing was cut short before it began. He left
behind in the glass ashtray on the arm of his chair the fag
he'd rolled but hadn't begun to smoke, so I took it away
and wrote a paragraph on that. 'The Martin Amis Rollup'
as I called my piece. 'Anything else?' Well, on the subject
of literary men, I was once in conversation with Julian
Barnes, who showed me an early draft – or rather plan – of
his next novel, a lined, A4 sheet, with just the heading and
nothing else: 'The World in Half a Chapter', something he

expanded on later, when the plan had progressed from blank to bank.

'You guessed it, Andrew. I could spin half a paragraph, and found lots to say, all of it substance-free. My readers love that stuff.' It seemed to cheer him up, as he saw as on a par the depth of his own journalism, pieces about the degenerated space surrounding the Guildhall, the town's flood defences, award-winning new builds on brown-field and riverside sites, carnival queens and the rest. I smiled gently and didn't contradict, but now the bar had closed. Wobbly, he climbed down from his barstool, adjusted his shirtsleeves, and made an age of putting on his jacket.

'Look,' I said, 'there's Louella. Why don't you walk her to her car?'

'Don't think so. That's someone waiting for her. I've seen him before.'

'Ah, him in a cape. Never mind. Goodnight, Andrew.'

8

The *Tribune* came out on Thursday, and on Sunday, when I bumped into him quayside, I mentioned what a fine gossipy write-up he had given Hoe's elite. I was with Lou walking Livia's dog, a Lab-pointer cross, a grey-muzzled elder whose lolloping, airy stride was the height of *haute école*, dressage an eccentricity I hadn't expected to see in Hoe.

Livia was Lou's Parakeet manager. She'd been called away to Cumbria, where her mother had grown forgetful

– midnight strolls into lake-filled valleys, in dressing-gown and slippers, with a cooking pot and box of matches. 'Great piece, Andrew,' I said. In it he named everyone but me, and loved Zora's little joke with her footmen and other flunkeys. He looked sheepish, but stood talking for as long as it took the dog to start to sniff his crotch. Mawdrie, the stand-off a faint smile and feeble gestures, twirled and retracted his hand, an action the dog took as play. No luck there. Mawdrie half-turned and was on his way to the Steam Tramp, with its cellar and carvery, as he always took an early lunch on Sunday. The dog was off in the other direction.

'*Bon appétit*, Andrew.'

Our walk was over an hour, its mid-point a bench on a bend in the river, the view a glebe, reeds and a sign in large block print stuck lopsided in the opposite bank, tidal depth or something. Dog-walkers all knew Lou and stopped to talk. 'You've settled in,' I said. I knew her through other work, having lifted bits from Horace Freelan's memoirs, a tome large in its chicanery, with Lou admitting she had ghosted it, on the basis of research a Commons hanger-on had made, eager with his *Hansard*. I lit my squibs under my *Bluffington* byline. I took the name Emoticon, and rambled in the mock learned way I had learnt, in fake admiration as to Horace's vision – at that time a Blairism already in eclipse. I didn't curb my tone when Louella paid me a visit, and sat demurely in my office. We hadn't met, but the name Ångström made me think. I got it finally. She must be the daughter of maths aficionado Edwin, one of whose

Cambridge books was set 'O'-level back in the day, though all I'd recall was a maze of simultaneous equations and a battery of x and y's. I asked who dreamed up the title, *Close Call* (back to the Freelan memoir). 'Oh, that,' she said. It had tripped out of her handbag so to speak, and Freelan liked it. A smile brushed her lips as she listened to what I, or Emoticon, had to say, that paywall construct scrutinising what captive she had pinned down in her pages, an ex-cabinet minister by the time she came to write. There were barbed asides she aided and abetted me in.

She had run her course with academe, she said, and was on the point of leaving her cosy office tucked away in the Tron Partick, or to site it exactly the Harald Fritzsch Building, an exterior clad with copper sheets stitched together courtesy some clever technicality (its engineering lost on me). The Tron Partick is famed for its research, and from the North Downs has road and rail links both to London and the continent.

She'd got property in Jericho (the one in Oxford), but didn't want to live there. I told her about Hoe's sitting MP, the garrulous Anthony Bliss, who puzzled at my fake résumé but didn't ask questions. I belonged to the overflow of London's disaffected, or so he thought – sophists mostly – ending up in Hoe. 'You go there when you're tired of London, not of life.' Okay, said Lou – she'd take a look. I didn't expect she would, but then one day she phoned and asked to meet, as I'd offered to show her round. 'Best place to stay,' I said, 'is the Pleiades. I'll meet you in the lounge. We'll take it from there.'

9

She walked round and up and down and shook hands with everyone I introduced her to, and that included Zora, who gave her the bridal suite – a masterwork of lighting. 'A friend,' I had said. Zora served us dinner on Louella's first night – a Caribbean special, hot but not too, gratis. Next thing I knew the Ångström name was linked with the Parakeet, at that time a dwindling low-ebb restaurant in need of a lift, with Louella looking at property. I kept to a distance. Not much happened once I had waved her goodbye, back to the North Downs, where in a last-minute clear-out she had problems with Bez D'Soon (a poet, a narcissist of course).

There followed months of on-off negotiation, Louella back and forth by train, showing up finally in the little black car she drove. I was up the Borné regularly, my magnet a twilit little emporium, Isca Collectibles, where I'd a fascination for the stamps, maps and numismatics – and noted the goings-on across the street. A scaffold went up. Men in overalls were in and out. Vans unlading blocked the road. The traffic raged. There were letters and emails to Anthony Bliss, affronts listed as a circular saw and the incessant bash of hammers. No sympathy there. Our Right Honourable friend stressed renewal as his watchword, and looked forward to a Happier Parakeet, with its swish new décor and Diggory's revival. First on his menu was black-olive calamari, a dish he'd invented, which even Mawdrie was moved to spout on about one Thursday. Then came the monkfish.

There was one other property too. Before the Parakeet reopened she bought a place on the moor and moved in. A removals truck had snaked an opening through the mists, knifing the hairpin bends – a caravan Lou closed off at its rear in her little *noir* car. I got something about it from a violist up at Stoneleigh, a tall, solitary, music theologian, his obsession Couperin (motets and other church music), and also Buxtehude. He'd been fool enough to go out walking on his own, without having mentioned – he was young and invincible – what his route would be. He looked at a clapper bridge. He bought postcards. He hiked. He had a huntsman's lunch in the garden of the Golden Dagger Inn, and read its leaflets. He saw for himself the place stark in its isolation, over 400 metres above sea level. Its prosperity diminished with the last mine defunct by 1930, while the inn was cut off completely in the winter of 1963. There was a Bronze Age settlement, whose remnants he thought he could just about make out from where he sat. He pushed a strand of red onion left from his lunch to the side of his plate. The weather began to change. The landlady, to whom he returned his plate and empty glass, warned against getting lost. But of course, he got lost. By nightfall the fog was thick, and all he could hear was an owl. Cold patches of light lit up that blanket atmosphere ahead, as he stumbled on. He followed the lure, and blundered into a rusty iron gate. That and a dilapidated fence were border on a scrub of garden, where cabbages had grown. He made out two figures talking animatedly (or so it appeared), shadowy outlines under an oblong of window light. Soaring rooflines disappeared into the night sky, in a twirl of mist, and there were other quaint features: stunted battlements, bits of balcony with pointed pikes for railing, bars, studs, iron crosses, machicolations. One of the two figures was hooded, caped, and heated in his talk. The other, a woman, responded sternly. The man cowered and retreated. The woman turned to the gate, and made out her intruder. Bruno de Roon, a musician she knew for his Buxtehude, having watched in rehearsal the de Roon Baroque ensemble, when resident at Stoneleigh.

'Louella Ångström, am *I* glad to see *you!*' He was lost, hopelessly, and on the point of panic.

'Come along. Follow me.' She led him onto a cinder track, a looping line skirting open country into a strewing of boulders. There was a gnarled apple orchard, tors as Bruno counted, and a final meander to Louella's garden path, and light in her kitchen porch. She took him inside. She sat him down. In the stark white of her scullery she plied him with coffee, then with brandy, then drove him – through lanes she hardly ever used – back up to Stoneleigh, an adventure I heard her side of when I sat down to pumpkin soup in the Happy Parakeet.

10

Swords, shields, bucklers, other weapons – tridents, daggers, scimitars – were put aside in Mawdrie's weekly debate, to date focusing on Hoe's five-star rating in the national transition league, towns linked by ley lines and other things hard to verify. The column roamed from hunt saboteurs to a fleet of rickshaws running up the Borné, driven by chip oil. As a change from crystals and crop circles the *Tribune* investigated the wind and solar farms and the hum of turbines up on Wedlock Hill, in a journalese dashed with coloured streamers. The dance was to tablas and panpipes. But there was no marriage of minds in change brought to the Pleiades, with circus acts up in the ballroom. First a magician, who took my mobile phone and pushed it – gone the laws of hard surfaces – into an empty Beck's bottle. I'd get it back, she assured – and I did, still working.

There was an illusionist, whose levitations no one understood, as he walked across the ceiling. A clean-shaven boy from Maryland, who'd majored in psychology, hypnotised members of his audience into acts on stage with partners not their partners. That had repercussions, with stabs of family revenge as I heard of in the pub. Round two was one-to-one with the hypnotist, with the whole historic cavalcade shaped in the person of Nell Gwyn, or Fanny Burney, or the Maid of Orléans, and not some calloused peasant no one has heard of. The thing gathered pace on Tuesday and Friday nights, on an eight o'clock start, with punters coming in from out of town, and paying over the odds for the Hoe-down catalogue of eccentricities. Mawdrie stopped going when he found it impossible to bag a seat, and I know for a fact wondered at the special allocation I could rely on backstage, with banter and shots of single malt.

Zora left it – her Pleiades biweekly – and me (with his special relationship) – more or less alone, and distanced herself completely, with Izabela dealing with the bookings. Months later Zora and I were strolling on a Sunday afternoon round the ruins of Burr Pomponia, cold and in need of coffee. I told her she'd upset not only the local gendarmerie, with cars double-parked and empty beer bottles in a multiple afterlife in the gutters round the Pleiades. The town's first scribe couldn't revive his lost authority now that our two Minervas were on combat terms, with each calling him to office and arming him with copy. By no means had he ventured into either inner sanctum.

I complimented Zora on her hair, which she'd had restyled. There was now a boyish fringe. The glint in her eye was its usual signature of diabolism, something I'd always liked. Not so her tempests, though I was ready for her outburst with the next piece of news I'd got. I told her to look more closely at Izabela's scheduling. A home spawn of capitalism's disaffected had made the last slot on Friday his own, when, dressed up *Clockwork Orange*-like (Kubrick), with a bowler and a radial pattern of make-up round one eye, he tinkled the keys of an upright, regaling us with belt-and-braces lyrics (or so you'd call them), lines intended as a slash at the 'establishment'. His accompanist played double bass, but at times he brought a saxophonist, at others a trumpeter. When solo he was solo. When an ensemble they were called Clump Left.

'This is something I need to know?'

'I think so, Zora. It's rumoured his next performance will be a eulogy to General Forsiss.'

'Oh, I see.' But she wouldn't shrug it off so calmly come next Friday.

11

Friday, the ballroom, ten p.m. Enter, left, Clump Left. Applause, anticipation. Bowler-hatted pianist screws eyes momentarily under sparkle of rotating glitter ball – a polychromatic flash. The saxophonist has been fired, and tonight's line-up will soon be the object of Zora's tempests. Its centrally stage-lit chelloveck has his two index fingers poised on the piano keyboard, or as multi-talented musician is about to prod at a rising-falling scale, still standing. His two droogs are a bassist and trombonist. The latter blows up to the ceiling and sprinkles over the audience a fruity flatulence at each spoken climax. He is well versed in the peaks in the manifesto the gruppa delivers. That precious document has been dressed in sultry couplets, vinegared, and comes out creech. Spotlight the piano malveck, whose end-stopped list is long. The PFI fiasco. Trillions in private capital shored up offshore. A disintegrating UK infrastructure. The banking crisis. A fraternity of finance CEOs picking at the carcass of Western ruination. Brexit (a dog's Brexit). Our NHS jewel sold off piecemeal to Tory donors. Diminished welfare. Immigrants get the blame. A sweatshop economy. Death of Greece. Youth unemployment. &c.

I sat with Zora backstage, she on a high stool with her legs crossed. For now I saw no flicker of discontent at that hammed up characterisation of the country she had fled to. She got one of her bar flunkeys to bring us each a half-frozen shots glass, on a platter, and wrapped in a starched napkin a bottle of Laphroaig, which she topped us from. As I predicted, the Forsiss eulogy began, with wreathes and tributes to his student ambassador, who with youth on his side had shot to fame at the start of the F regime. You know the name. Miguel Manuel Arango. You see his image on mugs and towels and tee shirts everywhere in the West. The duumvirate is upheld as paradigmatic, in standing up against imperial intrusion, at the cost of plunging its people into poverty ('The Heroics of Rags', as the song recalls). General Forsiss's achievements are a world-class welfare system and unbroken full employment, his two most salient points of departure from the West, with its marketplace payola.

I knew what was coming. Zora got down from her stool and flew off, enraged. I followed. She marched, perdition in that stride, to the front office, where Izabela had shut down for the day, and someone – one of her minions – handed the non-smoker Zora a vape, which she drew on furiously. I watched as she rifled through Izabela's drawers, but of course all bookings were locked up in her PC. She demanded the password. No one knew it. She called up Izabela, who had gone off to an ice show in Torquay. She relayed her login over the phone, as now Zora started up the PC, and pale with rage needed my help to find the bookings app. I got to the point of tagging Clump Left's future dates, which systematically Zora erased.

'Tell Izabela to make other arrangements.'

I knew what the Forsiss regime had inflicted on the Murillos, and saw with what vengeance Zora eyed those deletions.

12

Utopia, a one-time paradise, whose mainland is no more than clouds on a clump of trees, is not a day's sail from Thomas More's Land of the Didacts. In our case it's an actuality. It's visible just about. The best view is from the headlands and promontories of Cape Cold. Its last civilian president was Edmundo Morales, whose stake in pre-Utopia's brothels and casinos was solidly professional, though in unguarded acts of frivolity he took prostitutes two at a time to bed, or the most efficient of them. He dealt pliably with the mob's top echelon, far-sighted men whose returns (their investments were heavy) allowed an obedient Morales to siphon off a percentage for himself. He launched out on a programme where as President – in a kind of self-sanitation – he personally oversaw the country's trade deals. Enough were legitimate that as policy his image was splashed in the press on a regular basis, Morales a man of fat cigars and hearty handshakes. Business people loved him. Municipal workers and the less well-off were not so keen.

The first dissenting voice was General Guillermo Silva's.

His extended military service was seen as the right cachet for launching regular attacks in the press. His instrument of choice was the right-leaning *La Vanguardia*, pre-Utopia's leading broadsheet, with its supplements on sports and other leisure, and the country's fledgling fashion industry (one of those Western deceits strangled at birth, almost). General Silva was on the brink of retirement, so this was high-risk. His critique was from a military standpoint, focusing on one regiment particularly, its posting on the long desert border – hundreds of miles – where a string of barrios separated honest civilised folk from the jungle drug cartels, also secretly a part of the Morales manifest. With a distribution network out of pre-Utopia under mob control, and the President as puppet, Silva's homeland defence relied on an underpaid, under-equipped, ageing fighting force, which without renewal, and the modernisation of its hardware, continued to lose its war.

Silva was invited to the presidential palace, or mansion as it now was. It was pokey and inconsequential at the moment of Morales's inauguration, having four rooms apiece on its ground and upper floors, with its two storeys instantiated federal-style. One of Morales's first acts in office was its remodelling, using bricks manufactured onsite and a battalion of skilled, sweated labour. Added were flanking one-storey wings, to the frontage a grandiose portico, and to the rear a much simpler one. In warm sultry weather, as occurred most of the time, the front opened to the back, forming a breezeway. The whole is a thirteen-room bachelor pad and an example of Greek Revival, and is known colloquially as Los Pinos (for the shade of its gardens). On the day Silva entered he refused to be awed, impressed or intimidated. He looked up and round, expressing his admiration, even before he had got inside, pausing under the portico and its single pediment (for yes, the front entrance for him).

Morales received him civilly. The two men sat in the library, where the walls were a lining of polished leather tomes. Seating arrangements – the easy chairs and sofas – were studded Montana calf, cool to the touch and in colour maroon. The sun streamed in. The ceiling fans turned fast, noisy, monotonous. The two smoked cigars and were served coffee by a stealthy-looking youth, willowy and hazel-eyed, his movements stiff and robotic, and got up incongruously in a sailor suit, Victorian in its styling. He responded only with gestures when the President addressed him, slow, courteous, and painfully enunciated. Discussions opened with Major League Baseball. The atmosphere was filamented blue cigar smoke, in a swirl to the ceiling. With the pleasantries over, General Silva turned to the problem of indiscipline in the military, where he'd first-hand experience on border patrol, his posting unbearably hot by day, and cold in its desert nights. His men were suffering. Uniforms were wearing out. Boots had holes. Rifles had a tendency to lock, and the triggers jammed. Often hand grenades failed to go off. The troops existed on a diet of thin gruel and hard black bread, which you couldn't eat if toothless, as some of the veterans were.

In fact most were veterans. The only foreseeable outcome of all these deficiencies was a firmer foothold by the drug cartels, and a losing battle against them. 'Did you know their militia has better weaponry than ours?'

'That's irksome,' Morales countered, but then offered the revelation that without the drug cartels the pre-Utopian economy was likely to collapse. He deplored the brutality that would bring about.

'Well, that's certainly one for my memoirs.'

'I'd rather it wasn't.' Morales made him promise not to mention a word of their exchange, and in return he'd agree to concessions.

'Which are?'

The men would have new kit and a bolstered diet. All with a service record of over sixteen years would be retired on a pension – generous.

So the deal was done.

'And now, if you don't mind, General Silva, I have state finances to attend to,' in pursuit of which he expected, any minute now, the arrival of his advisor on overseas investments, whose special expertise was Wall Street. His name? M, or Em.

13

Zora knew that history, a first-hand agony for her, but comedic, banana-republic skittish stuff for me whenever it's reviewed. She frowns. I return a smile. You are safe now, Zora, I tell her. 'Don't talk about Silva,' she says, but I do and she wags her finger. I recall the fact of the General returning to his men, Silva tall in the saddle (a metaphor she hates). His convoy is led, flanked, and brought up by a deployment of outriders. Bystanders – peasant men with goats, women feeding chickens – were witness to the blaze of dust in the towns he and his orderlies passed through. By noon the following Wednesday he was back and calming his feral horde. He removed a glove and brushed at the layer of silt on his tunic. He reported candidly that Morales he had found a reasonable man, in need only of an objective account of life on the front. Only now had the President fully understood their problems. Promises were made, and things would improve.

It didn't stifle the mood of insubordination, however much Silva's put-upon, his defenders and front-line resistance, the first arm of the republic, were soothed. It was an uneasy quiet when three infantry kept a lookout along the supply line, where joy was short-lived on a plume of dust and a first arrival. Equipment included an assortment of ex-Bolivia boots, of all sizes – small, medium, large – and one new carbine for every four infantrymen. Whichever way you summed it – and the cooks and the bottle-washers did – once the footwear had been distributed, left over uselessly were tens, dozens, scores of pairs, all of them fitting no one. Half the men had to make do with what they'd worn before, down on their uppers. As for the firearms, when the cases were levered open it ended in everyone's disappointment (though Silva hid his feelings). Someone threw down the jemmy. Just two to three days' ammunition had been included, with the General certain more was on its way. There were murmurs, which gradually died down. The men shuffled off. By a fluke on the Friday a minor success was scored against the cartels, Silva's men peeling off into small guerrilla bands. Bonded by a new fraternal togetherness they dodged into and out of the jungle, startling the not-so-hated enemy in a return of its own tactics. Their advantage didn't hold. As punishment, on the stroke of midnight, one of the cartel bosses sent out his handpicked stooges, who dragged the nearest peasant farmer out of his bed and hauled him into the desert, where he was crucified. The palms were driven through with masonry nails, and the feet bound. The victim was given and shouldered a sign for Silva to see, 'THIS WILL BE YOU', in anticipation that normal cargoes north and up to the Cape – Cape Cold – would be resumed. The villagers, angry, demanded protection. Silva's assurances, as everyone suspected, promised nothing. He suffered defections – or desertions, to put it bluntly – when a handful of men crossed over to the cartels, where the lifestyle was relative luxury, and you did not have to gamble on a good dinner.

No other pledges were met, with no improvement in the diet, and no one pensioned off, Morales arguing he couldn't train replacements overnight (that 'overnight' stretching to a span of weeks and months). The men got drunk and did not leave their tents until after daybreak, sometimes ten or eleven a.m., with no reveille. When they did appear they were surly and insubordinate. They plodded round camp unkempt and unshaven, and took hours over breakfast, meagre as that was. The malaise spread further up the border, where General Forsiss was better equipped temperamentally, and did not delay in restoring morale, with an iron grip on day-to-day discipline. His rallying was soapbox-style and had the lacquer of speechmaking, with enough sheen that his most colourful passages were leaked to the press. *La Vanguardia* became his leading apologist. His two most sympathetic journalists kept a careful watch. He argued, popularly, and to great applause, that Silva's men had been given special treatment, when surely *all* border regiments could not operate on gruel and hard black bread. If one regiment couldn't do its job if ill-equipped, no regiment could. Silva heard these rumblings, and read the papers, if always three days late, for that was the time it took, his supply line still in disarray. He pondered his next move, always on the brink of mutinous ringleaders bursting into his tent and dragging him off – as the cartels had foretold – to meet his execution in the desert. His best tactic was to welcome Forsiss's voice as the best of all when added to his own, cheered that another iron leader (by implication his junior) had joined his campaign for improved conditions, with the ultimate goal a youthfully confident country and a people at peace with itself. Silva listened out, and construed in Forsiss's response no more than tacit acceptance of his leadership, as he flattered himself. He issued Morales with an ultimatum, which with prevailing conditions took days to arrive and meant a lot of hanging about.

14

Then came a momentous turn of events, which no one noted as such. One of Silva's men, out of tune with the moral collapse around him, kept to his discipline. He was stubborn – it was almost programmed into him – in the meticulous care he took, in the shine of his boots. He was mulish, obsessive, with the brassy sheen of his buttons, spending time on that alone. His efforts were supernatural, avoiding the least smirch to his uniform. It was spotless at all times, whatever terrain he marched through or filthy job he undertook.

He wasn't known for his sociability, and was slow, torpid in conversation, which with his low IQ (apparently) he found it simpler to shy away from. Then one day he looked pale, fell ill, and lay motionless on his bedroll, which was noticed, though no one commented. Then someone did comment, and tried to rouse him. He was motionless, cold, limpid, pronounced dead when a medic took his pulse, matter of fact about it. No one knew what to do, or what was the right procedure. General Silva got in touch with the Bureau of the Interior (or BoI), explaining that one of his captains, one of his 'many sad captains', had died, not in combat but of natural causes, and his family would have to be notified. So here was a curious thing. Whereas answers to his pleas for boots, carbines and a shipment of pork and beans were without conviction, an officer at the BoI made immediate arrangements for the body to be collected, that and its belongings. Silva was assured the relatives would be told. The speed of it bred resentment, and no one mourned when a field van arrived and the corpse was whisked away. Further, there was still no answer to Morales's ultimatum. Not a hat was lifted as a mark of respect.

The van, a distant speck, returned to the interior. Silva allowed a few days to pass, then used this incident, small in its consequence, as leverage into other requests for information. He made calls and asked after his loss. Would facts be made known after the post-mortem, assuming there was one? Could the family expect military honours at the funeral? The man was survived by a widow, yes? If not who would get his pension? Speaking of pensions, certain promises had been made to those of his men still living, and most were yet to be honoured.

There is no record of the subtle, sinister tone – the kind the BoI reserved for difficult moments – the General found that last inquiry blanked with. As he knew, the BoI parcelled up the country zonally, an official mapping everyone at the bureau understood. It seemed that on the border of Sc21 and Ti22 there had been confusion over the paperwork, and the corpse had been impounded. Important documents were forwarded to Nb41, but as those had become separated from crucial dockets held at Sr38, a release paper had to be signed before the body resumed its journey. Its ultimate goal was Cf98 – a long way off. The van had since been filled with crutches bound for the repair workshop (Tc43), and redistribution where needed. To add to the muddle, it seemed the body *had* been released (when it shouldn't have been), current whereabouts not exactly known. Further, in every direction you set a trace, the paper trail petered out. The dead man's people had ordeals enough, so none of this had been made known to them. It was hoped – it was devoutly hoped – they wouldn't have to be approached before it was sorted out. The BoI could rely on General Silva's discretion.

Well yes, absolutely, that was his watchword. Job done, therefore – for in the mist of this and other obfuscations General Silva did not press his one important point, the state of his border force, though he wasn't placated for long. Morales continued to ignore his ultimatum. Unrest and indiscipline on the desert strip threatened the full flower of mutiny, with Silva, aloof by nature, at pains to keep at one remove from his men. That made difficulties when it came to identifying ringleaders, though certain names were known to him. He thought about it endlessly. By night he downed slugs of American bourbon, and smoked too much – short, black, pungent cigarillos. He summoned his man Ortiz (Gregorio Ortiz), his trusted orderly, and under a blood moon, with cold portents, signed a secret dispatch, written in scarlet ink. That, under his fat dainty digits, he sealed in an envelope and addressed to *El presidente*. Ortiz was sent off in the dead dusk of dawn, and faced as his first problem a chequerboard of zonal disruption in the labelling he needed to pass through, not having the right papers to cross from Ce58 to Lv116. It meant backtracking through Pa91 and Nd60, and a revised route north starting at Db105. Ortiz did not lose his patience, and met these setbacks calmly and with fortitude, not suspecting that a team of operatives, its tentacles spreading outward from the BoI, monitored his every stride. It was known he had a penchant for boiled eggs and pickled cucumbers, so the obvious ploy was the placing of *agents provocateurs*, with a ready menu, in every *cafetería* he stopped at. It took little to get him to talk, munch, talk.

For all that he was barred on a back route – no more than a dirt road – on the jigsaw intersection of Ra88 and Fr87. With suspicion, armed police scrutinised his papers. Then, in a small wooden cubicle, he was interrogated, and ordered to state exactly what his business was. He admitted frankly he was on a diplomatic mission on behalf of General Silva, who had entrusted him with an urgent communiqué, that document to be delivered personally into the hands of President Morales.

15

Ortiz had that document taken from him and was told this was as personal as contact with Morales got. He didn't protest. He was frogmarched out of that little wooden hut and taken on a ten-minute hike – the barrel of something (a dummy weapon, as that turned out) pressed to the small of his back. He was led across a concrete quad.

He'd know it, and any square like it, from school days, for as usual it was bleak, treeless, powdery white – featureless in every way. An acrid wind was whipping through, funnelled by the edifice of old utility buildings on three of its four sides. Ortiz did not catch the eye of someone looking out from one of the windows, who turned away. That astute observer was occupied with the minute re-application of face cream, a recipe devised for his damaged profile – a long scar, a broad arc from jawbone to earlobe, on the left, on the sinister side. He inspected that work in his hand mirror.

Outside below him official cars were parked, among them a black sedan that had just been valeted. Ortiz's escort folded up and concealed in one of his pockets a wooden rule, hinged at its fifteen-centimetre mark – Fr87 standard issue. Ortiz was hooded and bundled into the sedan, which set off at speed with a screech of tyres, and took the hardiest route – cross-country over bumpy unmade roads. The journey lasted hours, but could have taken half the time. Ortiz, had he the presence of mind, might have counted all three checkpoints, alike with their barriers and the same wooden voices. On each occasion the driver needed only token gestures – the cursory wave of two travel permits, one for the vehicle, the other for its four personnel.

The car reached its destination, as now Ortiz had been brought to the heart of Fr87. His hood was removed and he was allowed to look. The team had parked up outside the presidential palace, that modest little mansion behind locked gates. It was, to Ortiz, a dazzling white in the afternoon sun, an intensity softened in the squat green shadows rising from the pine grove.

'You stay put.'

Ortiz obeyed. The driver's mate, shabbily uniformed, was handed the envelope Silva had addressed to his president. He marched to the gate and was met by a severe-looking youth in a white uniform and fur hat, English busby-style. There was a rifle on his shoulder, newly oiled. News was, no one now penetrated Morales's elite palace guard, which he'd gathered in greater numbers since receiving General Silva at his hermitage. Salutes were exchanged, but the gates weren't opened. Ortiz saw for himself the communiqué handed over, and was assured of its prompt delivery to *El presidente*.

'Now you go home. Tell Silva what you've seen.'

Ortiz was driven to a lonely patch of scrub where the dirt highway running east to west intersected with another north to south, and waited hours till a passing truck stopped and picked him up. So began his meander out from the nightmare and claustrophobia of Fr87, down to the gentle bucolic of border country, with is churches, dogs, chickens and crucifixions, having shown his papers and proved his ID countless times.

The General was furious when he learned of the off-hand treatment his envoy had been given, and the disrespect. He shared in the ferment of his men, who were won over by his change of mood. They were behind him when – as a sacred duty, as the patriotic thing to do – only thing left was a coup and a march on Fr87. They broke barriers. Overcame border patrols. They looted. They requisitioned council offices. Then when they got to the very throb of Fr87, a palatial playground in the shade of pines and bathed in sunshine, Morales had already packed up and fled. With the help of his Wall Street advisor – the scar-face M or Em – he'd siphoned billions from the pre-Utopia Treasury, now looking to his real estate in Florida, New Mexico and Hawaii, in a flip-flop between all three, planning his next move.

16

Confusion reigned, if not everywhere. A stickler for form at the BoI had united the disparate bits of paperwork – top yellows, bottom pinks, the transparencies – and matched their serial numbers with those marked on the drawers – coffinesque in proportion – somewhere in the parts department. The one, unique, defunct machine all this pointed to was got out and laid on the mortuary slab, and phone calls followed. I don't mean anything by it. I point out only one faceless bureaucrat in the upper echelons of the BoI, a carefully chosen operative with a good technical grounding in what each item of field equipment was meant to do, where it was deployed, when to recall it, and when to have it serviced. I keep at a distance. I call her X, or Exe, an inscrutable martinet, of a bony physique and the suggestion, faint as it is, of a masculine moustache. There. That's as much as I'm prepared to say (except that as a mole she reported to M. M and X, ham 'n' eggs).

She came down into the bowels of the Bureau's secret facility (it's right out on the edge at Lr103), and examined first the corpse, then the receipts. A new set of dockets – yellows, pinks, transparencies – she oversaw and signed off in standard-issue ink – blue-black, all that's allowed in the mortuary. The next journey for General Silva's saddest captain was as crated shipment to the laboratory of Dr Raphael Murillo, whom Exe knew covertly as the world's unseen leader in AI and robotics. Murillo, a family man, was among pre-Utopia's obedient servants, though privately he was not an enthusiast for the Morales regime, and had only a vague appreciation of Exe's undercover contacts. He did not know for example that a network had spread from the West as far as the BoI, though he knew Exe's position and had asked her for favours. He shouldn't have needed to, when on the whole *she* owed *him*, though of course this is politics, with its inverse laws and its undercover etiquette.

The corpse of Silva's captain was re-crated and labelled as an official BoI dispatch, overseen by Exe herself, who arrived with it at Murillo's hidden laboratory, where he knew what to do with it, but was ignorant as to why. He was told it was service to the state, and no more, and preferred it that way. I am sorry to be so cryptic. In time there are things I *will* reveal.

Murillo had married young. He'd long understood the brilliance of his mind, but was slow to uncover the gems that were there. The delay was down to constraints and interdicts on his youthful mental merrymaking, when he had somehow wandered into a labyrinth of colour-bland blind alleys, and was held back by groping, grasping, earnest PhD students it was his job to supervise. The problem, long-term, was a portfolio stuffed with the stunted advances the institution encouraged its students to make. It demanded much, and sapped his strength. It pinned him to a routine physically exhausting, and acted as a block on activities he found more interesting. With his arrival in the jobs market, that was the best of bad occupations open to him, all too pedestrian for a person of ambition.

He ran, academically, and was expected to do a share of admin, the computer science department at Fr87's Vespucci University – a treadmill. It wasn't what he'd studied for. As compensation he opened himself to a renegade canteen life and long coffee hours with others similarly captive – chemists, engineers, metallurgists, assayers in materials science, and a sprinkling of nanotechnologists (the whole leading edge). His bride Alejandra had grown up on another tack, through history, classics and music, and had won student awards, bursaries etc. for poetry and essays. Yet she too longed to get way, into the orchards of a freer academe, which both suspected might not exist, though the search seemed worth it. He told her one day yes they *would* escape, in the gabbling, breathless way he had, but secretly, *sub rosa*. He believed, he said, in brighter possibilities, and Alejandra took him at his word.

By some twisted miracle he stole time for projects dear to his heart, in a basement lab shared with those confederates listed above, whose joint plan had a long gestation and short evolution up in the refectory. Their first engineering feat of note was a robotic arm ending not in a hand, but pincers – a Meccano-like construction able to lift a pencil if placed on a horizontal plane – the first ever was Professor Murillo's HB. Trick was to rotate it through 360 degrees, and put it back down. A hand followed. After that a rudimentary eye, whose mess of wires and circuitry formed a virtual grid on a two-dimensional sample of three-dimensional space. Tests showed its content reimagined as a pixelated image – a bit blurred. With the increase in bpp values (bits per pixel) the image sharpened (of course). A stride forward, literally, came with a pair of feet, legs and a waistband, a slow, stolid contraption whose breakthrough achievement was a stroll across the laboratory floor and the ascent of two steps. Breathless applause. It had encore calls when after a sequence of failures it jumped a somerset, landing on its feet, its balance uninterrupted. At that point there were obvious possibilities, with Murillo inclined to dream almost into life an entire robotic being. The same paternal sighs were indulged in by one other on his team, a post-grad, who already thought laterally on *his* specialism – that being electronic language processing.

17

When their daughter was six Alejandra was offered research work at the Museum of Modern Art, New York, a career opening husband and wife were adamant she couldn't ignore. The getting of visas, a drawn-out process, designed to undermine, was an agony she overcame. She packed a trunk and left. Her absence gave Murillo the opportunity to wire up Zora's high-IQ image-factory, her brain, to a computer interface he'd got in blueprint. Data collected he uploaded into an electronic cuddly toy, complete with RAM, a furry thing with large alluring eyes and a repertoire of spoken responses. Prime among its conversational fragments was a Disneyfied 'Aw hello', and if it got no answer a 'No need to look so glum'. It could giggle. Students who prodded it on entering Vespucci's linguistics lecture theatre, where it stood on a pillar inside the door, had no idea who'd made it, or where it had come from. Murillo told no one. Nor did he mention his landmarks even to his wife. She wrote letters home, wanting to know how her darling Zora was getting on without her, with that as her one regret. It took the shine off the positive news of the work she was doing at MoMA (stimulating), and her apartment at Queens (confined if adequate, a bit pricey).

She shared living space with another girl, who set off every morning selling bagels, and in the afternoon lay on her bed, earphones plugged into Simon and Garfunkel, or Michael Franks, a sponge to her aches. Not quite to Alejandra's taste, who preferred mambo. She spoke excitedly of social and academic contacts she had made and enlarged on all the time. She was confident she'd soon find work for Raphael, as he'd love it here, this great open free country with its giddying, gigantic dream, its rewards for vision and self-reliance, so much of it tailor-made for a man like him. She so looked forward to the time when he and Zora, the light of their life, followed her out from Morales's den of vice, and they were together, a family again.

She wouldn't have known that every last item of correspondence was intercepted by a sinister someone – a pock-faced operative – skulking in the shadow world of the BoI. As intended Murillo *did* know, when the envelopes always bore the BoI's official frank superimposed on that of the US mail. Besides, those same envelopes – pale green and scented with Alejandra's Fifth Avenue perfume – were always torn open hastily and clumsily resealed.

He began to wonder if his letters in reply were also monitored, and had that question answered on receiving a visit, unexpectedly, by that sinister someone (above). He appeared spontaneously, an official carrying no ID, who asked politely if there was somewhere they could talk. Murillo met him in Vespucci's reception lounge, a cramped little space hung with a jostle of portraits whose production was nineteenth century. There his surprise visitor looked at home, a large man in a dull brown suit, baggy at the knees and elbows, with a face that hadn't survived its teenage acne wars. Murillo was careful to avoid his laboratory, where he'd got under wraps his first completed humanoid. On a command it could pour you a coffee but couldn't make conversation. 'Let's go to my office,' Murillo said, as that was several floors away.

They were served coffee by a live human being. Murillo stirred in his sugar cube. Talk turned dangerously to mother and daughter, Alejandra and little Zora, though the latter was growing fast. 'How is she coping without her mother?' Murillo said she was a bright child full of intellectual curiosity, blessed with enormous physical energy, and teeming with questions. The man from the BoI leaned forward confidentially. 'You can call me K.' He drew from an inside pocket a folded paper, where he'd a handwritten list of subjects, topics, opinions (political and economic) Murillo was not allowed to touch on – even remotely – in correspondence with his wife. There was, supplementary, a roster of names of people in the public eye he was also not allowed to discuss, with Morales and his generals featuring prominently.

'I am then being vetted?'

K only smiled. He was sure the professor understood, and thanked him very much for the coffee. 'No need to see me out. I've a good memory.'

That may have been so, but it was an hour, more, before he had found his way off campus.

18

Murillo didn't accept the 'K restraint' automatically. He schemed his resistance in the conferences he spoke at, with papers delivered at Vespucci's other campuses. His next letter to Alejandra was written at a furious pace and slipped in his luggage with his toiletries. His first (and only) target was his next quarterly visit to Sb51, a becalmed outpost of academe inland on a south-shore cliff, where the delicacy was goatfish, and Zora watched the vessels bobbing in on a green, sun-flecked, mesmerising sea. The professor went to his meetings. When he had to, he stood at the lectern. After, he answered questions. Less formally he allowed himself five minutes with anyone with the courage to stop and talk in the corridors (it's where the letter comes in). One evening, at dusk, he was on his way to a quiet dinner with his daughter, when someone – a dark-skinned, blue-eyed student in marine management – got him talking endlessly on the Riemann hypothesis, re some arcane theory of the pattern of decrease in salt-water fish stocks. It was a lively discussion. No conclusion was reached. Murillo said 'Nice to have talked' and made to go, but a thought occurred to him, and he turned. 'Have been trying,' he said, 'to post this letter for the past two days.' He produced it. Somehow he never had time to find out where the post office was – doubtless tucked away in a cobbled backstreet. 'Would you be so kind?'

'Of course. Leave it with me. Happy to help.'

All too elaborate, you think? Well, it was worth a try even if it didn't work. When Alejandra, the recipient, tore open this latest missive from home, she found large chunks of it redacted, strong iron bars in black marker a blot on certain clauses, or sentences, whole paragraphs at times, and must have wondered at the meaning. From that moment, on Murillo's side, he noted an abrupt change in tone in the things *she* said, most of it a flutter of inconsequentialities – trips to the department store, her confusion with the subway maps, traffic noise, the bland cuisine, where she went to worship. Nothing about her work. She couldn't wait, she said, to see them, husband and daughter – somehow or other.

Unsuspecting, but in all probability horribly anxious, Murillo took daughter Zora for one last stroll on the beach, and returned home. That was a two-bed apartment located on the third floor in a bustling suburb, on the corner of Simón Bolívar Boulevard, a tram-ride from school for her, and a short drive – against the flow of commuter traffic – for him. Evenings he helped her with her homework, her books spread out on the dinner table, as the city lights went on, and on the street below the restaurants opened their doors, and brought tables onto the sidewalks. Zora made short work of it (such a clever girl). With her year-long humanities project *she* taught *him*. He asked, and she told him again (and again and again) of the Byzantine philosopher, theologian and statesman Michael Psellus (1018–1078), whose melding of Platonism and early Christian doctrine prompted the renewal of classical learning, a scholarly strand threading the centuries and leaving its stamp on the Italian Renaissance. No small feat. Mawdrie has already shown us that

by age nine Psellus's daughter Styliane was tall, elegant, graceful in her movements, modest in her clothing, a girl admired by the rich and powerful, in whose company she behaved with artless perfection – no tricks, no boasting, all done without cosmetics. But she fell ill, with a plague-like disease, whose mark was fever and eruptions, and the ruination of her looks. She lay for twenty days with the pain of her sores. When those on her face improved her parents hoped for full recovery. But the fever worsened, and she'd no reserves of strength to resist the onslaught. She couldn't speak or eat. On the thirty-first day she raised her hands in a gesture of farewell, and after that the house was filled with mourners. At her funeral she was unrecognisable from that unspoilt beauty she had been, covered as she was in sores. Psellus and his wife were inconsolable.

Murillo reciprocated with his own extra-curricular material, teaching her to calculate in binary, octal and hexadecimal, and promising – almost daily – to show her round his secret laboratory, a conversation they treated as a game. When lessons were over and her homework books were back in Zora's satchel the real work began, Murillo determined to get them both away. He'd already sent off for his visa application form, a linked list with forward and backward arrows. A lot of jumping about, which for unknown reasons took weeks to arrive. Its ten pages of questions, the tone one of blame, interrogation, with demands for supporting evidence, were wilfully complex ('Have you ever, knowingly or otherwise, had interests in…' and a long list), with one false cross-reference likely to throw doubt on other answers given. He opted for a first pass through in pencil only – Dr Murillo's famous HB. When, finally, he had inked over every last dotted *i*, crossed *t* and open loop – the revisions, the precisions – he bundled the whole thing up in a manila envelope and sent it off, in hopes.

19

The reply was not immediate. When it came the professor was informed – the slant cruel, detached, bureaucratic – that he couldn't include his daughter on his visa, or anyone else. The most it permitted was a maximum ten days out of the country, for himself only. So began the Byzantine process to determine how he might acquire a visa for his daughter. There *was* a ready answer, tardily delivered. With so much recent unrest in the body politic the regulations had had to be tightened, and minors were not considered safe to travel (see Constitution, para 26, section vii, clauses 139a to 142b, on special powers and national emergencies). Murillo wrote to his wife. His wife wept, but didn't reply. He went ahead a second time with his visa application, and made arrangements for Zora's short stay at summer school, on the Golden Coast of Au79. The moment came, and with Zora packed off for fourteen days of canvas, camp fires and sleepless nights under starlight, Murillo got a taxi to the airport, with no one looking on, apparently. In other circumstances escape could have been easy.

The first leg of his journey touched him down at Orlando, Florida, where he brushed his teeth, and the second took him on to LaGuardia, where Alejandra met him. They shared a limousine with four others, and were dropped at Alejandra's apartment block, on 29th Street, near a demolition site, which made the daytime noisy and her furniture grey with dust. Her living space was small. They would have to find something bigger when he and Zora finally freed themselves, which to Alejandra didn't seem likely. She had read the unvarnished news in *The New York Times*, almost religiously. She was despondent, but didn't despair. She had made contacts, 'all sorts,' she said, and lots of people were dying to meet him – Harvard, MIT and Columbia professors. He'd get work easily.

They visited friends she had made. They saw the sights. They made their plans. Then, when his regulation ten days were up and Murillo was on his journey home – his soul stilled with reluctant hope – something, he felt, wasn't right.

He found out what that was when, almost two and a half years later, he made a second visit, Alejandra now living in a larger apartment in Brooklyn, on her own. She and a group of city poets hosted literary evenings, in the back room and terrace in the fish restaurant just a few doors from where she lived. Again he had come without Zora. Strangely she didn't talk about her daughter, though he knew she wrote to her regularly and dropped her postcards often (he had seen the images: Time's Square, Niagara Falls, the Rockies – views from Colorado and New

Mexico). It was clear she had moved on from MoMA, but she was evasive as to how and wouldn't discuss the work she did. She'd got better pay, and nicer things, and more than enough *Lebensraum* for one, and explained the change in fortune through investment advice she was lucky to have had. How so, Murillo asked?

She was vague. She had met, she said, a Wall Street journalist, a man whose scars in life weren't physical only, and who for reasons not understood had turned his initial, M, into his name, Em. Em had told her what shares to buy, and when – and when to sell. He seemed infallible. 'Useful,' Murillo said. She smiled – coyly, he thought. He said he was happy she had fallen on her feet, but then looked for other signs of Em in her apartment. There were gels and foam and disposable razors in her bathroom cabinet, for now with an enormous tub she had the luxury of warm suds whenever she shaved her legs – one further improvement on 29th Street, with just its shower. That dressing gown, with the tight blue checks, hanging on the back of her bedroom door – thirty-eight to forty inches (that's 102 centimetres) – 'Why, I bought that for you, darling.'

He was treated to Brooklyn's poet laureate round at the fish restaurant one evening. There was an audience. He scanned round those seated at the tables, and at those standing on the margins, subconsciously in search of a man with a scar. To his dissatisfaction, no one exchanged glances with his wife. He drank his barley wine. Green printed cards went round, signed by the laureate herself,

Murillo only glancing at his, and not reading it properly until he had flown back into Fr87, by which time he knew Alejandra had found someone else—

> Rogue organisms know
> How to unstitch, by coloured threads,
> This evolution we've been handed,
> Where impermeable walls collapse.

> What is left
> Is wholesale destruction
> And a tattoo certain of itself,
> Soundless in its concrete
> Layers of time.

20

Emotionally flat, he stood for half an hour in baggage reclaim. With each new item launched onto the carousel his expectations rose, rose, fell, plummeted, a sine wave charting the turbulent facts of his suitcase – a battered monstrosity, according to Alejandra. So what had happened? In its crossing from Florida and over Cape Cold somehow it had lost itself. It was nowhere. Then one very like it jostled by, and he made a grab. But he paused, and let it go, and watched, dejected, as its true owner swooped from across the hall, a large woman sprightly on her heels. She dropped it on a trolley and set off jauntily for home. As a kind of slow, deliberate torture, this little phase lasted until someone from airport security tapped him on the shoulder and uttered his name. 'Dr Murillo. Please. You will come this way.'

'This way' was a closed, unventilated, windowless room, where a man vaguely familiar sat at a desk, flanked by two security people, rigid in blue-grey uniforms, immobility written into their features, their faces a shadowy crosshatch. In Fr87, peaks of the caps were low on the forehead. There was a vacant chair, hard and straight-backed, opposite his interrogator's, who motioned with his finger and told him to sit. He did so.

'I am K.'

'Kaye. You are not the first to have turned an initial into a name.'

'I'm sorry?'

'It doesn't matter. We've met before. What do you want? What have I done?'

K had one of his operatives heave Murillo's luggage from under the desk and onto its surface, that same beaten-up antiquity the sophisticated Alejandra had shown horror at on seeing. K had already been through it thoroughly.

'I've confiscated the two bottles of Jack Daniel.' He enunciated painfully slowly. 'They should not have gone in the hold. Where is the duty bag? You are supposed to declare at Customs.' No response. 'You are an intelligent man, Dr Murillo. I would expect you to know.'

Murillo said he was sorry.

'And here's another thing.' He produced the Brooklyn laureate's green card and waved it briefly, with a hint of critical triumphalism. 'I have been struggling, Dr Murillo, to know what it means.'

'To be honest I haven't read it – or not that closely.'

'Well, I am no Derrida, but let us both do that now, you and I.'

'You are educated, K.'

'You do not need to humour me.' K bent himself – head, shoulders, the whole upper body – in a sedulous pose over the Brooklyn poem, with a Biro hovering. Its title got him started, 'Geological Separation'. Therefore we must attribute to that simple nomenclature primary responsibility for the opening bout of clumsy deconstruction on K's part, whose college years had been a pepper of French philosophising on the logos and its meanings. 'Geological' was so obviously code for 'political'. That cast a penetrating light on what followed. We see in 'rogue organisms' social activism (or so said K), and in the unstitching of coloured threads the long-established patterns of the state undermined. The words, phrases 'evolution', 'impermeable walls', 'collapse', are first indication of the march of the marginalised, on the long walk to power, periphery to centre.

'Are you part of that march, Dr Murillo?'

'That is ingenious, K. But no.'

He hoped not, as no one on hallowed turf south of Cape Cold wanted to see that 'wholesale destruction' stanza two so glorifies, with a last tucket of republican authority cynically buried in concrete. But K was wiser than that, knowing its specific aim. A lot gets carelessly lost from a nation's collective memory, oversights useful to poets and newspaper people, given the accretion of lost decades. And of course, decades in political life are tantamount to the enormous wastes of geological time. That much you see in the gnomic outpourings of Brooklyn's poet laureate, which in the final analysis are grimly forensic, which is a paradox. Or as they say in the philosophy faculty, an antinomy.

'I wouldn't know. Literature is not my line of work.'

'What is your line of work?'

'Engineering. I am an academic. I supervise PhD students.'

'You are an academic at Vespucci University. AI and robotics. We have been hearing things. We are watching.'

'And you are…?'

'We are the BoI.'

'I see. Is that all? Can I go?'

'What's the hurry, Dr Murillo?'

'I am already late. I have to pick up my daughter.'

'Don't worry. Zora has been taken care of.'

'What do you mean, *taken care of*?'

'I said don't worry.'

'Are you letting me go?'

'Yes. From now on you will report to me.' K gave him a card, with K's official contact details on it. 'No need to go through the case. Everything's there.'

'Apart from the two bottles.'

'I will put them in a customs bag.'

'Thank you.'

'You will co-operate.'

21

So. Murillo reported to Kaye, Kaye reported to Exe, and Em looked on from Wall Street. $M = xk^2$. Upshot was Zora grew up under the shadow of that equation, while her mother pined. Alejandra showered her with gifts, the essence of maternal love resolved to a list of things that survived the US mail – that was the first obstacle. Second and much more formidable was K's scrutiny at the BoI. Confiscated, as might have been the fate of the doctor's bottles of booze, was a small library of vids and CDs, as far as K was concerned the explosive phantasmagoria of America's decadent culture, where the singer is a screechy sort of sex symbol, and the film doyen is raffish, unshaven, is penile with his gun, and is etched in popular hashtag 2A consciousness, the true upholder of democratic norms.

Zora's little museum collection consisted of a garish orange-coloured box, now emptied of candied fruits, a toy trumpet the size of a thumbnail, a ten-dollar bill she chose not to exchange for pesos, birthday and Christmas cards, rings, necklaces and bracelets without value as jewellery, but of great sentimental worth, pieces for her hair, a sewing pattern, photographs Alejandra had taken herself of a bakery, a Gettysburg memorial, a kosher butcher's frontage. There was a vast collection of handwritten letters, the talk couture and vegetarian recipes, and pages torn from a fashion magazine, and a shoelace (significance unknown). Books by Erica Jong never made it, while I suspect K never got past a read of the jacket blurb. But never mind – because Zora was not in need of someone to help with her escape. She'd manage that herself. In relating that history (to me, and doubtless to others) she stressed the one exit she would not emulate was the one propagandised in Western political psychology, with its Oedipal prince – a forlorn, tactile soul awash on the tides of Viennese id-isms. She preferred instead a reversal of the myth the centuries had meshed him in, as at last he unstitches its fiction and stumbles blindly *out of* rather than back again into family bondage. What Zora valued was clarity, and not that ancient, clouded, masculine vision.

Her father understood, but quietly somewhere removed. When she enrolled for her baccalaureate he told her to bear in mind that the lecture theatre was not quintessentially a place of educational exchange, or the dissemination of aims and ideas, or much of it intellectually arrived at. It was tightly bound in institutional propaganda, of a different brand for her generation than had been for his, which he summarised as obedience to the state. For the student today it masqueraded as the inculcation of a north Europe work ethic, with that in itself presented as an act of cultural appropriation. The country had to be built. The same vigilance applied to whatever reading list she was given, whose political purpose she was urged to scrutinise as closely as the texts themselves. The academics who'd authored them were subject to the Professor Murillo litmus, and were found wanting – blinkered individuals absorbed in personal standings set against the social-academic upward slippery slope, a scented gradation the power-hungry always looked to. But Zora knew it already. She had pored over Roman and Byzantine history when not out on the yard with her skipping rope. Armed so, off she set, into a soft environment shaped to overturn the body politico – the *dolce* contra the Duce – or softer than her father's. Murillo's office and secret laboratory had always been in Vespucci's central campus, close to the estuary, the River Maestra, where the dockyards and little engineering firms were the bend of his horizon. The humanities faculty was steeped in garden vistas up on the northwest edge of Fr87, where Zora strolled alone through the cork palms and butterfly jasmine. Her essays weren't of the mantras her teachers wanted, but as Murillo's daughter she couldn't be marked down, or not seriously. Top grades were always out of reach, but she hovered just below – and took it as a moral victory.

Murillo looked on with approval, Zora a natural in the political manoeuvring the acquisition of academic honours demanded. He reflected and smiled tightly on how he had never read Alejandra's missives to their daughter. He respected private worlds, nevertheless he thanked her, *sotto voce*, from the bottom of his heart, for what was shrewd, sound, motherly advice (or must have been). When Zora had time on her hands he showed her round his laboratory, a menagerie of sure-footed synthetic little creatures, whizzing in, around, and out of wickedly complex mazes. On the shelves was the scaffold of dissociated limbs, their extremities closing a prehensile iron grip, able to simulate the musculature the Darwinian universe has made necessary for moments of sudden flight. He'd got a ghoulish, human-looking skull – a millennial relic – inset with manufactured eyes, its entire ocular wired to a dedicated processor, and with it a computer screen showing us its depth of vision. The skull allowed its naked jaw to drop, the mirror to our astonishment. 'Impressive,' said Zora, though she hadn't yet seen Dr Murillo's fully functional humanoid.

He co-opted her, by mutual agreement, into his project. Once she had graduated – and with trumpets, fanfares – she spent as much time working for him as she did in Vespucci's little Eden, where she burrowed into the postmodern façade in her fledgling role as researcher. At that seminal moment she was starred for an all-conquering career as feminist cynic. She plumbed the depths of what was said to not exist – history – to 'prove', as she said, that yes, it didn't exist, while nor did facts. Then perversely she'd dredge up ancient texts. To that extent she played the game. Among her achievements was a translation of Jonson's *Sejanus*, for the first time revealing that learned exposition as open to a single exegesis, in terms *only* of power and group identity, as it shifts from one to another. She located in it seeds of destruction the institution wouldn't have seen as its own, and the kind of destruction her seniors didn't approve. But that was Zora, an animated spirit of Janus's doubled purview, all entries written in a calendar of Januaries. Her retrospect on the Elizabethan and Jacobean stage pinpointed on it a catalogue of entrances and exits – nothing more.

22

Not only had Zora graduated. For months there were official distortions on the news and rumblings apropos of General Silva. A rise in discontent at the margins and at the fragile desert border was attributed – but only for so long – to lawlessness, and the obstinacy, the insularity, of an ignorant peasantry. Now Silva had made his glorious entry into the capital, where not to his astonishment alone Morales wasn't there. The ex-President had pilfered the nation's silverware, and was off on a short vacation, summoning an invasion force while combing through his swag. Silva promised an end to that all-pervasive corruption the ousted regime had been built on. He did his best to ensure Morales's end would come in the rule he had mimicked, when in its last embers Roman republicanism gorged on its depravity. His first act was to take control of *La Vanguardia*, in a careful 'realignment' of its editors, with state control of all other media next on his list. His promise to his people was a brighter day ahead.

Murillo, his arms crossed dejectedly, stared out from the open window in the small living room of his and Zora's flat, where a street party had begun on the boulevard below. The pallor of early-evening lights went up, a pearly opacity. Shade trees lining the sidewalks were filled with coloured streamers. Fireworks got under way, purple starbursts a dab of blurred oils in the fast-flowing Maestra. Car horns sounded all over the city. In the bars glasses foamed, filled to overflowing. Zora said that many of her friends were out celebrating, and she was off to meet them when she'd had her shower and put on cooler clothes. In reply he was quiet and still and ill at ease, but didn't object, telling her only not to be late – prone as he was to lie awake at night and worry. 'Don't forget,' he said. 'The 22 tram. It stops at midnight.'

A useless appeal, as at three a.m. Murillo lay staring at his bedroom ceiling, in a fretfulness that threatened its paralysis a second time, just days later when the officious Kaye dropped in on his lab unannounced. Zora was there too, working with Murillo on what was his definitive AI architecture, a circuitry expanding exponentially, into a universe it took a second pair of hands to get under control. He was older, and felt the fatigue, and was vulnerable at a concentrated level of design, where Zora was suddenly more adept, and kept a tight rein on the reams of code they had written. She brought to the workbench instant recall – a catalogue of systems routines and the tasks they performed, so many Murillo had begun to forget. There were acres in her stride where *he'd* begun to plod, as between them emerged new exotica in the manipulation of human-sounding phonemes, machines given an authentic-sounding voice.

As Kaye prodded round, picking up, turning in his hands, and putting back down bits of equipment he didn't understand, signs of a breakthrough were kept from him. Murillo hedged round his answers with questions put. Kaye tried to correct him: 'I am not the enemy.' They talked about Silva and the new regime. Who could say where that was going? Said Kaye: 'It does not affect the BoI. The state runs as it runs, and we all do our work.' Zora covered a contemptuous smile. Murillo indicated by his look that he did not want her to speak. Kaye got to the point of his visit. 'My boss wants a meeting. Exe. You know of her. You will be ready at nine a.m. tomorrow. A car will call. You will bring your assistant.'

'She is my daughter, not my assistant.'

'That is not what we have heard. Nine a.m. You will both be ready.'

The car that called was a Jeep in battle camouflage, its livery clouds of green and brown, with remnant twigs in its nets. It sounded its horn on the boulevard below at 8.30, while Zora was in the bathroom. Murillo looked down from the window, then at his watch. That half-hour ploy had got him flustered, while Zora, standing at the living-room mirror with the hairdryer, watched him gather the wrong documents to his briefcase. At five to nine she had corrected his errors, and safely filed all she deemed too sensitive, and led the way downstairs. The Jeep's two occupants were uniformed. The driver, excessively polite – obsequious with Murillo – escorted Zora personally to the back seat. The other, senior in rank, showed he was armed, a gloved hand fondling the leather holster on his belt. He sat in the back with Zora. Murillo was shown to the passenger side at the front, and climbed in tentatively. He did not like the conversation that began behind him, Zora quizzed as to what she had studied up at Vespucci in the Garden of Eden. Her brief was culture, philosophy, history

– or let's just say the humanities. What then was her interest in her father's work? She said only filial duty while she waited for certain papers to come through, as only then may her real career begin. 'Oh, and what was that?' She referred him to an answer she'd given before, as she regarded (obliquely) the presence beside her. Let's just say the humanities. He changed the subject. There was a wide choice of lively nightclubs on Simón Bolívar Boulevard – he wondered if he'd ever see her at the one he frequented. She did not gamble, she said, and had never visited the casinos. Cabaret she might enjoy if not for the crooners. Her interrogator wasn't satisfied: 'I hope to persuade a change of mind on both.' Dr Murillo twitched, but did not say a word.

Their journey left the public highways, with a dirt road entered via a barrier with two-man checkpoint, where the driver – also keen on boulevard nightlife – flourished special papers. There began a tedious slog on a long stretch of macadam snaking through Fr87 savannah – fine yellow sand, on each side endless wastes flecked with the burnt brown of its undergrowth, scorched if drought-immune. A haze on the foothills remained as distant however many kilometres the Jeep battled or beetled through. Zora looked up and away from the shade whose hand was almost on her knee, and followed a black hawk high above trembling on a thermal. Murillo was visibly out of sorts so soon as that depopulated landscape became a scouring of uniformed men on exercise. Live rounds. A dilapidated tank. Puffs of oily smoke.

At sight of no sign or signal the Jeep veered off onto a dusty track, its course an extended loop, 180-plus degrees, ending on a small lot enclosed on three sides by low-rise flat-roofed buildings, where Exe had just been on the phone to Em and was looking through her office window. She watched that improbable quartet step out of the Jeep, with the two she had summoned marched politely into the reception area. She adjusted her fiercely pressed lapels, and probably touched her hair, and stepped across the compound, and found her two guests uncomfortably seated close to the water cooler, showing no interest in the rack of papers and magazines. Her attempts at friendly normalisation, with handshakes, a smile, a warm welcome, all seemed to work, with Murillo relaxing immediately, and Zora curious as to what it was all about.

'All in good time,' as Exe was fond of saying. 'If you will just follow me this way.'

23

The severe, ascetic Exe, in her forced attempts at lightness, led them through a labyrinth of gloomy corridors into a stale-smelling, clammy coolness, an underground chamber Zora assumed was the morgue. You cannot blame her. A porter already waiting put away his newspaper and hurriedly stood to attention. Exe directed him efficiently to one in a bank of drawers, which he opened. With her help he lifted out on its stretcher and laid out on the mortician's slab the serviceman General

Silva had repatriated at his death. Murillo recognised the unit he had made adjustments to and shipped back to Exe. The porter was dismissed, and went off with his newspaper. Zora watched as, with alchemy she'd never seen, Murillo revitalised the cold cadaver, dark round the sockets of its eyes, stiff in its uniform (boots down at heel, as previously noted). Murillo had an app on his cell phone, whose outline imaging made critical sweeps of the droid's anatomy. With each phase he went through, the eyes blinked open, and the hands began to exercise themselves. On an elbow, the thing lifted itself up from the waist, then dropped its two legs down dangling to the floor. Colour suffused the cheeks. The hair – wiry, matted, tangled – took on an ad shampoo's vitality. When asked if Murillo could make it stand, he made it stand – a ponderous nobody swaying gently in the fetid air, and speechless. Its creator, who'd had no idea of its deployment when first signed off to the BoI, knew from its dress, from its uniform, what this first among his units had been used for. He did not like it, while of course Zora was fascinated, and dumb with astonishment. Said Exe: 'Can you make it talk – again?' Murillo said he could, but that had always been problematic. 'This as you know is a prototype,' he said, 'and by present standards its conversation algorithm isn't adequate.' The corpse, new life trickling through its veins, listened intently.

These were new revelations as to her father, Zora looking on in puzzled appreciation at what took place, if slow and laboured. Exe had questions. She asked Murillo's automaton, now brought back into the circle of the living, what was its name, where was it from, did it have family, et cetera. Each answer was lacking in spontaneity, and required intense consideration. Murillo said that was an illusion, as the thing had no powers of reflection. All it could do it did on the basis of heuristics, recursion, imitation. It achieved its goals – simple things like tying a shoe, or boiling a kettle, or driving out to the highway – as tasks it had learned from authentic human beings, and that took precedence as the most productive way of doing work. A machine endowed with the plasticity of human flesh and blood, as Murillo contended (and showed his political colour) was a social liability having no moral regard for other forms of life. That lesson we must have learned in a glance back to the first stirrings of industrialised Europe, where the workforce, brought in from the fields to the factory, had a life forced on it as enslavement to machines. Exe agreed, we could not disregard the hazards, but as a resource – it trumped any other talked about worldwide, and was invaluable. Murillo cautioned. There were other drawbacks, with serious implications. For example he had produced no unit yet able to distinguish between foxes, wolves and huskies. A human figure planted on an arctic background was interpreted differently from the same under a tropical sunset, and fiddling with variables, in an attempt to correct the deficiency, led to unintended consequences (too technically specialised, Murillo argued, to bother her with).

'Nevertheless, Dr Murillo, this is an outstanding achievement.'

The tall, pale, stooping dummy subject to so much scrutiny, flagged visibly and sat back down on the slab.

'Not yet fully recharged,' said Murillo. 'There are ways we can speed it up.'

There was one other thing he could help her with. Her department was under pressure to download what visual and audio information the unit had gathered while on deployment, but there was no one left who knew what to do or how to work it. There had been a clear-out, and resignations, and uncertainty, and with the last days of Morales lots of reassignments. Murillo said he'd shipped the unit with a user guide. A section explained what apps were available, how all gathered data were protected by encryption keys, and how apps, data and keys fitted together. She pledged him to send another copy, and organise a day of training. She would put her best technical staff under his supervision, and draw up a programme. To Murillo's agony, these were strictures bound for collision with other plans he'd made – though as ever the problem was Zora, who must flee the country before him.

24

Lots more phone calls, and Em less free to move about the country than before. Exe told him she'd got what she wanted from Murillo, and was working on the girl, Zora. She'd got the language thing not exactly cracked, but a lot less limited, new units betraying less of Murillo's engineering at low-to-mid IQ. 'If you get my drift.' Em drove over to the compound, slowing to a crawl as a mark of respect for his friends on exercise. There were landmines, and live ammunition, and a burnt-out tank. He was fully apprised by the time he stood with Exe in her office, poised to help when she took in a second unit on recall. Silva would have known it as the boy who served coffee and lit his cigar on his first negotiation with Morales. Morales was still not aware that his procession of call girls, those he prinked and petted on the velvet of his sofas – the prelude served with an ice bucket, before getting down to business in his boudoir – was now on record. Em and Exe chortled at his small talk. Also there for replay was Em's detailed commentary as to his spreadsheets, and advice to Morales on how to invest his plunder once the General had finalised his coup.

The General had finalised his coup. So, after our detour, paths cross again. There have been car horns sounding on the streets. Fireworks. Bars, clubs, open all night. Exe and Em have shown their hands (but the trump card one of them keeps concealed). The rumour now circulating was of Silva having subjected the senators he'd inherited to rigorous examination. Where feasible he fired from office anyone unlikely to retaliate, doing so on grounds of corruption. National security was everything. His spies were everywhere. Conversely, he'd had enough sense to keep his civil service, and for now no one at the BoI was threatened with expulsion. Nor had the General decided whether or not to make the palace his official residence, complaining to one of his aides (quite bitterly) that its largest bedroom, with its balcony and pacifying view, reeked of sweat, blood, faeces and semen, and couldn't be used until the fumigation people had been in. Exe had moved swiftly in the hiatus, recalling – as we have seen – the lackey droid stationed with Morales as his Man Friday, but known as Alfredo (I do not record what was decided on as surname). Alfredo or Al Friday Exe was intent on reprogramming, endowing him with an ailing grandmother, an old biddy holed up in a southern shanty town, so giving him good reason to absent himself, or, to be exact, to reveal from time to time what was going on in the General's household. But now Exe and her team had hit another problem, with downloads out of Alfredo working as they should, but uploads not. 'I am going to have to get Murillo in again.'

Em suggested one last try with the user manual before resorting to that. Exe acquiesced, but her best technician got nowhere. There was no choice but to bring Murillo back, this time without his daughter, in whose absence he seemed more nervous than ever. He fiddled with his apps, confirming yes, for some reason no uploads seemed to be possible. He identified the board he thought to be at fault, located in the torso and consisting of a set of circuitry he reeled off unrepeatably as strings of alphanumerics. There was only one firm he knew of able to repair or replace – AI Vogus, in Santa Clara, California. The drawback was there were huge problems getting the right clearance. Sending anything out of the country was a tortuous, bureaucratic process that always took him months.

'Don't worry about that,' said Exe. '*We'll* handle the clearance.'

And so it turned out. A few days later Alfredo was delivered under escort, sealed in a crate, to the Murillo laboratory, which was now relocated to the Garden of Eden. 'You'll enjoy more privacy there,' as Exe had advised.

Before Murillo had peeled off the bubble wrap there was another delivery, this one arriving with an official flourish in the hands of a courier, who would not leave until the manila envelope he had brought was signed for, a sweep of the pen he scrutinised without lifting his visor. Zora, who grew suspicious, in trying to get him to do so offered iced tea before he left. He thanked her very much, saying no, he had to get on, but took her on a stroll through the avenues, across the lawns, the grass there coarse and newly clipped, and out to the margins, where outdoor décor was a riot of shortleaf figs and begonias. A low ornamental wall separated off the concrete lot where he'd parked his bike. She had a message, she said, for Exe, as he mounted. Her father had suffered much, and did not deal well with the stress he was under. 'I will pass those observations on,' he said, and on a wisp of exhaust departed.

Murillo had more reason to worry, now that, to some extent, Zora had broken free – was never home for dinner, and was out most nights till three, four in the morning. Whatever the day of the week it was, it made no difference.

Pre-emptive, she'd rehearsed her answer, practised in its flippancy, though the question was never asked, what she was doing, where it was she went. Fact was she had taken up that offer on their car ride over to the compound, and spent her nights sipping cocktails in the casinos and nightclubs, careful with how she mixed and blended in with Fr87's criminal fraternity.

25

Em flew back to Wall Street, and resumed his cover writing for the *Post* (or the *Bluffington*), with his dollars' worth of wisdom on the rise, fall, rise of the Dow, his specialism. His editor wanted more on crypto currencies – were they a good bet? – and a lay guide to their supporting substrate. From down south Morales wanted new investment opportunities, and phoned him endlessly, and was impatient at how long it was taking assembling an invasion force. Em apologised. 'We must wait,' he said, 'for the next banking scam.' Failing that, public outrage at the trillions in debt sapping any last vitality remaining in the West, or whatever uplifting subject. He reiterated how important it was to bide one's time, or wait for just the right hot topic. You had to be careful in the choice of rhetoric, as the wrong sort would attract rather than deflect public attention. You did not want the press swarming with hints of a counter-coup, especially as it now had imperial backing. 'And remember, it's still in its planning phase.'

That blueprint Em already knew would have to change, with the coup Morales setting himself as counter to now running into trouble. You might think to the victor the spoils, though the only spoils General Silva found were a threadbare Treasury, a spiralling deficit, the threat of sanctions, and a loss of overseas aid. Not only were the other generals restless, it was harder to get his propaganda funnelled through the *Vanguardia*. He pulled off theatrical tricks when in promising to 'drain the swamp' he got rid of Morales's toadies still in the Senate, a thinning-out with at least one serious consequence: much of the Senate's day-to-day work couldn't be done. He kept quiet about the war on drugs, having to admit Morales had been right – the economy would finally implode without the cartels. Best popular target was the casinos and bordellos, which officially he closed but privately allowed to trade on the black market. Zora knew all about it. With that flicker of intelligence masked by her poker face she gambled and accumulated.

She'd got friends in low places. Her father didn't know what she was doing when she spirited away those clearance documents Exe had sent on, insurance of Al Friday's passage to AI Vogus, California. She was aware, too, there were other firms he used in Texas. She hung on to all that important paperwork he knew not why, for over ten days, Murillo at great pains bit by bit (byte by byte), disassembling that faulty Friday unit into its component parts. He packaged each individually, and put the whole lot in a warehouse crate. The lid he did not staple into place until he had gone through his checklist, no more than a matrix of blue boxes he and Vogus had come to understand each other by, each mark-up showing what circuitry needed to be replaced, and what serviced.

Where, he asked Zora, were the crucial bits of paper? She was matter-of-fact. 'Only a few days now,' she said, and stuck by her word, producing them without explanation. When an explanation was what he wanted Zora was evasive. 'Let's get this stuff shipped off,' she replied. Murillo threw in his checklist and sealed the crate. The all-important dockets were taped to the outside. Miraculously, in just two days Vogus had taken delivery. His instructions were followed, without mishap, and with like efficiency the repairs were shipped back to his laboratory. He put it all back together, and having dressed it in a dark blue boiler suit got the thing standing, walking about, able to say its name. Exe got excited and sent someone over immediately to collect. 'Our technical team has got pretty *au fait* with the user guide,' she said, for which she thanked him. It was a polite way of telling him he wouldn't be told to what use Al Friday would be put, though of course *we* know. He'd be sent to work as before, wherever General Silva decided his official residence would be.

That initially was the palace, but the president's problems were mounting. He'd begun to hear of General Forsiss – a rival he had met often, though not as a friend – who with Silva's rise, and in the political vacuum left on the desert strip, had worked up his oratory all along that borderline. According to the front pages delivered daily by the *Vanguardia*, he had got the troops behind him. Worse, a charismatic student, in his last year at agricultural college – where else, in the militant southwest – had begun to make incendiary speeches, mostly to the converted. You could see his picture all over the press. His name, Miguel Manuel Arango.

Arango was popular copy, a Messianic figure, articulate and photogenic, his image destined for mechanical reproduction all over the West, on coffee mugs and tee shirts, the look having resonance in all areas of protest. *El presidente* – for so Silva had briefly restyled himself – felt the first twinges of panic, and instructed his man about the palace – Al Friday – to gather his office files and pack them in a trunk. Of course, Al did as he was told. A few days later *El presidente* reverted to martial order, again calling himself the General, and drove in convoy to Fr87's central barracks, where he'd a third-floor suite newly cleared for himself. He selected from his ranks a new praetorian guard, as permanent protection. He would need that insurance. He instituted a proliferation of parades, and from his office each morning looked out on the files of men he was due to inspect, determined to ignore the frantic phone calls put through on his private line. The news was always bad. The economy was shot. Revolution was in the air. In the chaos Morales was coming home, backed by the imperial enemy into whose arms he had flown, an enemy not at all pleased at its commercial losses here in its casino playground.

26

Forsiss ensured one of his men was present at Arango's next ascent of his soapbox, which took place on the town square in Puente de Piedra, a hamlet that had grown exponentially. The place was famous for its joinery and the engravings on its obelisk, the names and dates a roll of military heroism. Arango's flights of demagoguery were fearless, and got the crowd cheering. He did not stint on the sarcasm, telling his eager listeners how their new president was as narcissistic as the last. There were hoots of derision when, having got it on good authority, Arango revealed – to the last *real* almost – the millions Silva had poured into his image. Soon we would see him, cast in bronze, astride his horse, in every town and city, raised on a marble plinth. Public spending otherwise diminished on a daily basis, and continued to do so, and that got everyone incensed.

It got a glowing report when news got back to Forsiss, who made up his mind to be there himself next time. The next time was deliberate in its provocation, given the venue Arango chose, a barrel house in the River Maestra delta. In its lead-up was a march through central Fr87, with banners and klaxons. Arango knew just how to manipulate the multitude, a detail not lost on a fretful General Silva, who sent in armed police, their brief to break up the meeting, having overplayed the threat of violence. The target was easy, a mecca of mercantilism the vast unwashed had descended on. Arango spoke at length, and was cheered. A stone was thrown. The military bared its batons. There was a pistol shot. The crowd mutated into a horde, and in its rampage broke down doors. Neighbouring property was suddenly fragile, solid, padlocked buildings in reality vulnerable, no longer secure. There was looting, which Arango took no part in. Instead he found himself swept up by one of Forsiss's men and driven off at speed to a safe house, bewildered and asking questions. No answers yet, amigo.

Some of it made headlines the following day, with a scurry of sub-editors newly ambitious at *La Vanguardia*. It confirmed a resurgent ideology, and spoke for the elites, predicting a government crackdown more swingeing than the last. Forsiss read the news and later said how pleased he was. He went off in secret to the dingy little apartment, its blinds permanently down, a three-room place out on the margins, where his new ally was holed up, and told him the revolution was unstoppable. For two days his diet had been beans and black coffee, but Arango was modest, objective. The question was, how to turn an angry mob into a well drilled administration in waiting. Forsiss had his views on that. He knew the several fronts he would fight on, as now he recruited Arango as first man in his embryonic Ministry of Information. 'You mean propaganda,' said Arango. Yes, exactly.

Forsiss took him off to his military outfitters, where he tried on a face veil, fingerless gloves, a dun-coloured crewneck jersey, terrain boots, lots of different combat trousers. He modelled himself before a full-length mirror, and, finally, was unable to decide on a side canvas bag. In the end he took just a khaki dress shirt, and in accompaniment a green cap and a red-star beret, with the latter – as all of us know – destined to be his trademark, that image beloved of Clump Left and its blinkered little leader, whose entertainments Zora cut short in the ballroom at the Pleiades. But that's to jump ahead, or back.

Arango stuck with his khaki and the starred beret when Forsiss, who made available a Jeep and a driver, gave him what facilities he'd need in tearing upwards in an ever-closing arc along the desert strip. He set off early one morning. At each new encampment he slept under canvas – 'those sacred tents', as he called them – and warmed up his oratory preaching to the troops. His route was south-east-northwest, ending on O8's coastal town and also its capital, where the industry was kelp and fishing. He set up his stall on market day, and with his torrents of spittle and brimstone – a biblical spectacle, even in that conservative backwater – got hoots of support and a ring of hats thrown in the air. His barbs were aimed at Silva's broken promises. The imperial enemy still ran our interests, with its mob culture and its laundered thefts, and remained the control-ling hand in our institutions. If corruption had gone away, so should the casinos, and the bordellos, but they were thriving more than ever. The Coca Road still ran south to north, with its cargoes unpatrolled, and crossed the straits unimpeded. Our friends at *La Vanguardia* knew it very well. Worse, *El presidente* had probably sanctioned the major distribution points, for the journey on to Cape Cold and its icy waters. From there who knew where next – the hellholes of Los Angeles and Chicago. That got honest, hardworking folk puffed with rage.

The Forsiss masterstroke, timed to coincide with an Arango at his rhetorical height, turned out not to be. He was forty, fifty kilometres north, with a band of sixty men, primed to attack the hill fort of Monte Leña, a geo-political co-ordinate important to Silva symbolically. I like to think that the precise moment Arango took his cheers was when Forsiss closed in recklessly, having underestimated in what numbers Silva's men defended the fort.

27

The Forsiss catastrophe unfolded irresistibly the moment he swaggered into the study up on that O8 hill fort, the shady retreat where Silva had written his presidential speeches. He liked the cooler temperatures as well as the furnishings. The settees were a plush morocco. F thought the commotion outside must be his band of cutthroats putting Silva's last defenders to the sword, but the door closed behind him and four of Silva's *flics* stepped from the shadows. One of them spoke – with good old-fashioned sarcasm – and with a snarl of satisfaction rather than awaiting a reply. Forsiss, about to speak, got for his insolence a pistol-whip. Together with his eight outside – all that were left of the sixty he had brought – he was cuffed and sent for trial at Fr87. He appeared before his judges in manacles, and wore an orange jumpsuit.

Arango was at the trial, with a shorthand copyist, who

with diligence set down in a lined notebook the list of charges (sedition foremost). The case for the prosecution was embroidered calmly, methodically. After that an impassioned defence, where Forsiss trusted no one, relying on only himself in pleading his case. It was a flourish lasting ninety minutes, and wore on into the long shadows late in the afternoon, a controlled tirade that saw his accusers twitching for the gavel. Arango made much of the small fact of Forsiss straying off script countless times – a script he'd rehearsed in his cell – and proclaimed joyously how he, personally, Arango, could never question his leader as to why. That volume of notes he'd had so scrupulously written down was expanded into a cache of A4. From there the Forsiss student of revolutions crafted the F manifesto. Arango sang it on the streets, his first outing timed to coincide with the start of Forsiss's twenty-five-year sentence, when he slept long, kicked his heels, and read the papers. That restless activity was at the southern tip of Tm69, in a secure unit, where the barred window, an icy ocean, and the snowline on the horizon, meant no escape.

Arango visited often, with news from the world outside, its focus his first-hand perspective on the drudgery of daily life. Not much of what he said was reported in the press, that instrument of propaganda now under paternal super-vision, the best euphemism yet for state control. The peo-ple knew it and were angry, and showed their frustration in a groundswell of support for Forsiss's failed coup. There was talk of an F movement, the direct result of Arango's manifesto circulating everywhere. He said to his leader, 'Do not despair.' He brought books for the General to read, with advice on rank and importance: Gramsci's *Prison Notebooks*, and as close second his *Letters From Prison*. Added later was a new translation, with introduction, and a system of annotations replacing original footnotes, of *Das Kapital*, and for lighter moments a superficial arty scholarly look at the tortured world of Hieronymus Bosch.

Forsiss got on with his reading, aware only vicariously of his nation's unrest. People brought their protest to the streets – marches and rallies. It turned ugly sometimes, and required a military presence, with batons, the full panoply of riot gear, and as last resort water cannon. Each day ended in a cavalry charge, with injuries accounted to both sides. Rocks were hurled, and marbles fired by a boy with a slingshot – a David against Goliath. The point arrived of civil unrest as an almost permanent state, when Silva – barricaded in his barracks – blinked and lost his nerve. He invoked executive powers, intervening into the judiciary, with Forsiss's sentence quashed, and the verdict pronounced unsafe. Forsiss was released immediately, and was shown on television with his green cap and wispy beard, in eager anticipation of the work ahead, of forging a brave new state. He added how grateful he was to President Silva for the opportunity to play a part in that supremely sacred task. As you may guess, he'd learned his rhetoric from Arango.

Silva offered him a role in foreign affairs, which after days of introspection and a tough round of negotiation –

it lasted into the night – he accepted. Silva thought it had got him out of the way, with Forsiss blazing off on luckless errands into the imperialist heartland, flights interstate, the tour bus city after city, or failing that spurious missions further afield – but actually no. He said he'd use his diplomats for stuff like that, prime among them Em (or agent M), whose remote presence moved him, inexorably, into Kaye's proximity, then Exe's, or as is said here K and X, or as Forsiss called it the MKX axis. From that moment on you could not tear him away from matters of the interior, with Arango perpetually at his side.

28

That cuckoo in Silva's nest spread its wings and made itself at home, and not without subtlety. Forsiss's contribution to cabinet meetings was delivered with calmness in its authority, without aggression, and was crafted so as not to challenge *El presidente* confrontationally. It ran counter to his views nevertheless, and stunned others first into stutters and mumbles, then into chasms of silence. In time that could not be interpreted as other than dissension, a departure fully aired when Forsiss prevailed eventually. As Arango predicted, he had won approval and support, because, of course, he was right, 'rightness' the central tenet of all ideologues, who lacking the sharp penetration of self-scrutiny are certain of themselves. Silva skulked away and pondered with the light off in the twilight of his office, still unaware of who was watching, and listening, and of all the little devices planted everywhere. He summoned those most loyal and of his protectorate, one by one, and by the same quanta (singly, as they shambled in and out) discovered they were not so faithful after all. The game was up. It was time for him to go. The country was in turmoil. A fresh start, please. We thank you for everything you've done (which wasn't an awful lot). Goodbye and do not take it personally.

He gathered his last papers and batched them in his document case, and agreed. Now was the time to take a rest and write his memoirs – what a tale he'd tell. His friends smiled meekly and saw no danger in that undertaking, and even spread the rumour he had packed some overnight things – his favourite toothpaste, some aftershave his niece had given him – and was off for a few days. Forsiss stood in, naturally, by common consent. When next Silva was heard of he was guest of former president Morales, at one of Edmundo's health spas, a poolside emporium he'd acquired in Key West. Timed to dampen these ructions was a series of addresses Arango delivered in the capital, and repetitively in major towns and cities, his sentiments reported in the press, with passages clipped for radio and TV. His picture appeared in glossy magazines. Not known to him yet, he was given film-star treatment in an icon-hungry West, whose modernity is ranked with history's brackish conurbations, a bit dismal really, always eager to dish up a running revolution in its full force as mass entertainment.

Arango, everyone's pinup boy. He was careful in his

idolatry of General Forsiss, and dreamed up just the right distortions on his family background. The new president's father was described not as a wealthy farmer rooted in the agrarian nobility, but as a man of his country's soil, in close connection with its people. That cradling was further massaged in its humble, kitchen-table detail, the boy Forsiss shown as hard-working with his schoolbooks, and with the help and encouragement of both parents winning a scholarship to Vespucci, where he studied law. The law, as perhaps counter to intention, sharpened his morality, in the first place sprung from honest family toil, and now fully formed as the vehicle of his rule, Forsiss the only proper successor to the two previous incumbents in the office of president. The Forsiss investiture Arango referred to as a done deal more or less. We did not need an election. Forsiss gauged the response. No cracks or fissures appeared. He went public himself and set out his plans. All foreign-owned business he would nationalise, and repatriate its alien proprietors. Silva's half-hearted attempts at stamping out vice and corruption he personally would follow with something swingeing and incisive. The roads were a mess, he knew from experience, so Forsiss was going to have the potholes filled. He intended a new chemistry for the country as a whole. To start he dispensed with that zonal system mapping the nation (uninspired as it was, for bureaucratic reasons the BoI stuck with the ease of its grid).

The first city given a proper name was the capital, Fr87 now known as Eutopium. By extension the country it was capital of was referred to as Utopia, at least popularly. Pledges Forsiss gave his people were summed up by a *Vanguardia* journalist – a shorthand promptly used by all – as the F regime. The F regime scored a high percentage in the promises it kept. Crowds came out and lined the streets and cheered, as trains of Americanos, effete and pampered colonials, their families in tow, scuttled off to the airport, trunks hastily filled, billfolds too, but forced to abandon the source of their payola. If what they left behind couldn't be nationalised, it was abolished. Handkerchiefs were waved, and not a tear was shed, with hoots of glee the last verbalisation on the last farewell.

Forsiss was adamant that he and his country wouldn't relent, and saw, in retaliation, a raft of sanctions imposed from overseas, with states large, middling, small, keen to gang up. The economy dipped. Interest rates rose as buildings crumbled, prey to a powdery residue in the salt air sweeping over Utopia. Nationalist pride refused to be dented, the children of the F regime plunged into short-term fixes – a patch to the roof, darned socks, padded knees and elbows – temporary holdings in reality long-term in their solutions. Public services wound down, but not the health system. That in its full florescence was available to anyone, anywhere, at any time, with money splashed on hospitals and local surgeries, and the recruitment of doctors, nurses, midwives. Everyone over fifteen had to be a car mechanic, with the transport infrastructure thirty, forty, fifty years in rust, and vans, sedans and charabancs – jalopies of every corrosion – kept going, and somehow going. Then at eighteen you worked an allotment.

29

Forsiss gathered intelligence wherever he could and by whatever means, and in it read its opposites if he thought he was being deceived, which happened often. In all he trusted his MKX. That continuum had reliably drawn up the same blueprint for invasion as had landed on the desk of the deposed General Silva, who for strategic purposes had teamed up with the playboy Morales – Morales, who on a whim wanted his tropical playground back. They'd got an army behind them, a ragbag of ex-business people Forsiss had expelled, a sorry elite whose NRA ethos and a sense of entitlement were no preparation for its exploits ahead. Landing craft were multiple – of how many vessels reports vary – and were targeted on Utopia's northwest coast, Truffle Bay to be exact. Forsiss guffawed and sucked on a cigar, waiting without trepidation, as under a new moon, and a starless sky, a highly untrained invasion force got itself caught in the marshy inlets, and instantly knew its bad choice geographically – cold glutinous mud swamping every hapless footfall, an ooze into every stride. Commendably no one tried to surrender, perhaps no bad idea. Forsiss's men either picked them off – the ease of it as target practice – or picked up the stragglers fleeing for the coastline, where the boats were already in flames. It was a spectacular conflagration, though I have no supporting photographs.

Forsiss rounded up these despised enemies of his thrusting new state and paraded them through the streets, from Central Square to his military courtroom, which didn't have to session long in reaching its verdict. Insurgency was punishable by public execution, though Utopian lenity commuted that outcome, and the sentence was custodial, with no prospect of release, and a diet of gruel.

'Your president may try to intervene as he wishes, but the talking should have come first.'

Their president did try to intervene, with ludicrous assassination attempts. Zemblan, Gradus-like cut-outs were parachuted in to carry out and ultimately botch up that 'reconnaissance', to use the official term, as I echo diplomatic discourse. Em witnessed one such effort, a drive-by shooting as Forsiss stood on the steps of the Senate, having delivered in that chamber – to a concert of heels pounding on the floor and a cascade of applause – his first state-of-the-nation address. A boy masquerading as a water-carrier pulled up briefly on his motorised rickshaw. He pointed the revolver intended to end the F regime, but his hand trembled, and his aim was poor. He rode off in a swirl of brown exhaust having winged the shoulder of a cameraman, who in the press of international journalists was jostling for position. The cameraman survived. The boy did not. He was found, tried, hanged. Justice is remorseless. Other essays on Forsiss's life are too numerous to list in full, but here are some. The poison that sent his food taster into a paroxysm resulted in the minutest scrutiny, the most zealous analysis and step-by-step monitoring of the supply chain ending in the presidential kitchen. There is an account of the brake pipes severed on the limousine Forsiss did not take, but a chauffeur delivering flowers on his ma's ninetieth birthday did. He paid the price for that filial act of devotion in plunging over a corniche and meeting his death in the emerald rocks and the shoreline spray below – a smoking wreck. Other smoke without fire was in the box of cigars delivered – supposedly one leader to another – in a wrap of pink tissue to *El presidente*'s desk – a joke surely, as the first one he lit blew up and blacked his face, though did him no lasting harm.

Forsiss, in tightening his grip, called back the tireless Arango from his circuits of propaganda. Together the two laboured long hours, pausing only for the suppers they were served, and drew up a checklist. It traversed the alphabet from A, an accelerated review of security, to Z, a zodiac of home surveillance, with the entire population under observation. The F regime had Forsiss's insistence that dissension he – and the brute force propping him up – would not, could not tolerate. We enter an era like something out of Solzhenitsyn. Citizen X might one day be standing on a street corner discussing baseball results with the friend he'd bumped into, Citizen Y. A black van draws up kerbside and X is bundled in, driven off, and his wife, workmates, employer never hear of him again. Y lives his future in fear of the same. The structures of rumour and supposition plant *a priori* in every adult mind the nightmare of interrogation, orchestrated by the state, and carried out in an archipelago of labour camps. If you had once, at any time, anywhere, said anything counter to party doctrine, you began to live in fear of the midnight knock.

Yet still Arango was the exemplar of peace, freedom and human flourishing.

30

Murillo had friends who had gone the way of X, and colleagues who'd formally answered questions. Nights his neck was tense on the pillow, as he lay plunged in the half-certainties half of dreams – bitter and elaborate ill-staged things – and half as the wakeful overseer dreading the after-midnight knock. What had he said? And when? And what hadn't he done? And why?

Zora had perils of her own. Her flirtation with Eutopium's criminal lair hadn't ended with the rise of the F regime, or the bark of its zealotry, or its hatred of the rich. She saw as well as any when it rounded up the pimps and usurers, and drove them out. She told her father not to worry. The people she hung out with weren't at all bad. Those she brought home – sometimes, as a rarity, for sugary drinks and a round of cards – were not what he thought. Murillo judged by the crease of their cloth, by the cut of their hair, witness as he was to a dazzle of circus garb, with bizarre-looking hairdos, multi-coloured quiffs and other bits tinted, a harlequinade that had taken him aback. Their aims were much as his, she said, in an underpinning whose only lack was education, the great vacuum forming the shape of their activities, always short of means. 'Hope you're right,' he said. Then one day there did come a knock, in the calm of a Sunday afternoon, a gentle rap on the front door, repeated when Zora looked up from the coffee she was stirring, and Murillo crumpled down his newspaper, tentative, afraid. Zora swapped her mug for a vase she had emptied in the sink and was about to wash out, and went to the door clutching it. The two she opened it to were half-intimidating – this a chapter of halves – the short, barrel-chested one, who smiled and habitually cracked his knuckles, dressed in regime green, but not the first to speak. He left that to his partner, a tall man with a stoop, dressed in a business suit, and scarred from ear to jaw on the left profile.

'You are Zora Murillo....'

Zora didn't respond.

'It's your father we'd like to speak to.'

Murillo was standing, ashen-faced, with his back to the picture window, the leaves of his newspaper cascading from the coffee table, where he had dumped it, to the floor. Zora barred the way and held up the vase above waist height as the two started to cross the threshold.

'No need for that, Zora.'

The tall Em ran his thumbs up and down the sharpness of his lapels, while the other fingered the small Beretta concealed in an inside pocket. Zora relaxed, and let them in. The preliminaries were got through quickly – no sitting down, no coffee, no nothing – Zora told she had to stay put. It was only Dr Murillo they wanted, and if the professor was ready....

'I will just put on some shoes,' a brown pair down on the heels.

'I'm coming with you.'

'No. You not come.' Again the Beretta.

Zora watched from the window as the three left by the street door and crossed the boulevard, where in a line of parked antiquities, on the street's opposite side, not a van but a black, gangsterish saloon – with rounded bonnet, rounded arches, a lot of chrome and running boards – gleamed in the sunshine. Em ushered the professor into the rear, where cordially he joined him. The other pulled a bunch of keys from his trouser pockets and took the wheel. That old Chicago vintage shuddered into life, and after excessive manoeuvrings out – a jolt forward, a jolt back, wheel hard right, and repeat – the thing sauntered to a stop at its first red light, edged across a yellow box, then zoomed on in triumph up to the highway. Zora, the phone already in her hand, strained from the window, as she marked its fork left and its final disappearance. Murillo asked calmly where he was being taken, and Em – who moved in a mysterious way – said all would be clear in time. No attempt was made to prevent the professor noting the route.

Whatever that route was, the car never left Eutopium. Its only brush with officialdom was at the barracks where the F regime had made its headquarters, as here the barrier was manned by members of Forsiss's guard, one of whom lifted the pole when Em flourished his papers.

The car was parked in the yard, in a depth of shadow slanting off a low-rise warren of offices, to the door of one of which Em escorted his guest. The driver melted into the background. Forsiss was seated at his desk, an oceanic oak expanse whose only objects were a box of cigars and a photo portrait, the likeness of whom Murillo could not see, as he stood before his leader. The frame was silvery. Its backing was of stiff black card, into which was cut a complicated stand, which held the whole at an angle. There was a long, unpunctuated sentence handwritten on it, in red ink, a scrawl he could not decipher, with a date. He relaxed momentarily, in an atmosphere subdued by its twilight, tawny in its tinge, with a stream of sunlight pouring in through the blinds Forsiss had drawn behind him. Forsiss stood up in a staged smoothing away of the tension in his brows, booming a friendly welcome. He shook, with vigour, the good professor's hand – 'Or shall I call you Raphael?' With a nod Em was dismissed, and (supposedly) heard nothing more of their conversation as he backed himself discreetly out of Forsiss's office. Murillo sat down when indicated to do so. Forsiss flicked open the lid of his cigars, but Murillo said no, he did not smoke. I imagine Forsiss sat back in his chair as he mentioned the carafe of lemonade he had ordered, which duly arrived, on a tray, and with it two spotlessly clean glasses and a gift-wrapped biscuit apiece. Murillo crunched on his uncertainly. Forsiss munched away. He launched out with warm words and nothing but praise for his predecessors, while admitting Morales's only fault was in not facing up to one, glaring, obvious fact. Viz., that the country's problems could not be solved by civil government alone.

By contrast General Silva had seen it as a self-evident truth. Forsiss had thanked him – heartily, fraternally – for laying the foundations of a healthier, happier Utopia, as now there were brighter days ahead.

31

The F regime's achievements were a catalogue, a pillar of the nation. The last of the north's foreign owners had been deported. What monies they had not had time to salt away were flushing through Utopia's restructured economy – a people's economy. The south was next. There had been a massive clean-up in the nation as a whole, with a crackdown on gambling and prostitution. That had seen the jailhouse filled with the racketeers and pimps with a monopoly on those trades. The result, recorded crime figures down to their lowest. Anent the welfare system. The F administration took it seriously (a point in its favour). Education was next, an institution surely meant for the many, not the few. Forsiss had enlarged its ministry, its brief to bring us knowledge, learning, training, as a universal right. Nothing, he said, would stand in the way of the F regime, whose authority was hallowed, as Murillo knew from the arrests he had seen. He did not ask what had become of those fleeting simulacra, men and women here with us one minute, vanished the next. Subject to 'gentle' persuasion, in all probability, having refused to part with secrets they didn't possess, and allowed to rot with the pimps and racketeers. Let that be a lesson.

Forsiss was philosophical. It was a sad fact, as I heard him say repeatedly, that problems long overdue for fresh ideas couldn't be solved without expanding the prison system. Regime F profoundly regretted delays in similar pioneering endeavour for the education of its children. As everyone knew, weaponisation preceded humanisation. Murillo showed that he understood, and tamely drank his lemonade. Forsiss sat forward, on the creak of his chair. 'In thirty words I will get to the point,' he said, and so it proved. The remaining challenge for the regime was the extent of its desert border, or incursion over it by the drugs cartels. What had that to do with Murillo (a question he did not ask)? *He* was just the technician, but between them Forsiss and Arango, they were the vision. Both had been given scintillating reports of Murillo's quietly run laboratory, and both felt full force the waves of national pride in the world-class work he had done in the field of AI and robotics. His master now commanded: Murillo, and a team of his choice, would take charge of a secret facility in a secure location – a Utopian Area 51, as was whispered confidentially – in the production of regiments of automata, whose sole function was to police the border and defeat the cartels. Forsiss reserved a more sinister tone in relating how he'd heard great things too of Murillo's daughter Zora – for oh what a gal – she an A-star student trained in the classics, but boasting an aptitude for software engineering. 'Of course, we will place her at your side.' I imagine a leer, and Forsiss raising a single eyebrow, and Murillo pressing on with his lemonade. Murillo tried hard not to show his alarm, and even pretend how honoured etc. That outpouring Forsiss took as a sign of how humbled he was.

Murillo took the news home, silently. He was dropped at the same spot he was earlier driven from, and strode an undeviating line across the street and up the stairs. Zora was in. He sat her down at the dining table, where she had placed a vase of cultivated gerberas – a yellow, pink, and orange effervescence – before telling her what it was the President pressed them to do. Not all bad, he added, as the money would be good, and Area 51 (as he'd decided to call it) promised them an ultra-modern complex extensive in its reach. Zora asked him what he'd negotiated in return – paid flights annually, concessions to leave the country, the possibility of reconciliation with his wife Alejandra.

'No, none of that,' said Murillo. His impression was they had to do as they were told, a point put to him with the nicest coercion. The unspoken truth was they had been co-opted into fitting out an invincible army the F regime might as easily turn on its own people.

Said Zora: 'We must plan our escape.'

32

Murillo admitted it was almost impossible, at this juncture, not to go to pieces, something his daughter told him not to do. She kept him at their little two-place dining table, with its embroidered cloth and centred bouquet, and its view from the window, where Murillo's anguished gaze had fixed itself. 'Concentrate,' she said, and bullied him – as only his daughter could – into recall, a review, the sober contextualisation of everything Forsiss had said. 'Begin.' She had a pad and pen and made a list: last of the north's foreign business people gone, and assets seized; the south next; the puritanical purge on gambling and prostitution; racketeers, pimps, incarcerated; the drop in recorded crime; welfare, a box ticked; education ditto (or as is said currently, a noble aspiration); the F regime unstoppable (but Zora would see about that); as bureaucratic exercise, dissenters rounded up and taken off the streets....

'Now, take me to Area 51.'

Murillo did not have the authority to do so, and had no clue as to where that top-secret, government complex was exactly – somewhere in the desert, with a water supply, and truckloads of stuff arriving daily. It didn't matter. Zora's plan was two-pronged, and – as no end of his despair – meant continued contact with her reprobate friends, or those swanning round the underworld, where in a sleaze of diminished lighting she had sung her way past the son of Nyx, and could get what she wanted. What she wanted was documents. Then in anticipation of father and daughter's new work in the desert she acquired a white lab coat, with a patch pocket for pens, pencils and screwdrivers, a box of tight-fitting gloves, fluorescent in their colouring – cerise, purple, yellow – and a hairnet. The net, and the way she slicked her hair, made her into a martinet.

The image suited her needs when at last Forsiss greeted them – *père et fille* – at Area 51. Lots of military personnel

– blank-faced automata whose composition was genuine flesh and blood – were stationed at points various round the compound, and demanded ID even on entry to, and exit from, the maze of narrow streets servicing the residential quarter.

'Yes, you'll be stationed here for weeks at a time.' That fact Forsiss conveyed as the last authority able to conjure human freedom through a programme of honest toil. He was cheered at how earnest the two of them looked.

Living space was a composite of sandy-coloured cubes bronzed under a hot pulsing sun, the windows small, square and barred. Each allocation amounted to a galley, a bedroom with single divan with space for a chest of drawers, a sitting room with views across the dunes, and a bathroom with toilet and shower. Ventilation, in all rooms, was inadequate. Zora made it clear to her father that she for one would not be here for long, and nor should he.

'But what can be done?'

'Plenty,' she said.

She put herself in charge of the production line. She walked round efficiently carrying – at Forsiss's insistence – an old-fashioned clipboard, which at intervals absorbed her meditatively. She played her part as she stopped and sucked the stub of a pencil, and made a mark – a cross or a tick – in the great matrix her operation had been reduced to as paperwork. Murillo, who acted the role as Forsiss had come to think of it – of boffin, an archetype all of us understood – did as his daughter instructed, secreting himself in the quiet of his office, its décor a plain ivory, working at his latest schemata, the design of a next generation, or Utopia's ultimate enforcer. In truth he frittered away his hours eaten up with nerves, and relaxed only when Forsiss left the compound, his motorcade a glitter of chrome under plumes of desert dust.

Zora had a second, secret production line, its work interrupted when (those code names please) K and X introduced a fresh intake, every third day, Sundays excepted, when half a dozen BoI operatives, youngish men and women keen to learn her programming skills, sat in her classroom in gazed awe and honest wonder at her new machine. It was her one compensation, the only jollity she was sensitive to confined to desert life, Zora straight-faced, straitlaced, waspish, a schoolmarm after all, all power in her hands as she held captive class on class of eager civil servants. First thing was how shrilly she impressed, as a kind of refuge in the technics, in the duolingo of babble and gobbledegook, when as preliminary she gave her impenetrable account of hours, weeks, months spent slaving over her father's automated phoneme manipulation – for behold, a robot brain able to process language and respond when spoken to. She had made it seamless, natural, and that was the Murillo achievement, father and daughter. And yes, the great man himself would be paraded before the whiteboard – a surface cratered with equations – the moment the class had graduated. In truth what she taught did not introduce them – not even the brightest – to the minute arts of microprogramming, as instead their only concern was the user-friendly front end cloaking those convoluted processes accumulating within. Nor was there a droid at their disposal, but only the bit of circuitry – guts spilling out and naked on Zora's bench – relevant to them, a network of interconnected pseudo-synapses taken on trust as the Murillo language processing board. She told them to open their laptops, as now their work began with wireless access to it, while in no sense did it seem an anti-climax. Only thing her dazzled pupils worked with was a simple text file, whose entries defined the being you wished to create. Excerpt here—

```
%whois%
$sex = male
$forenames = Luis Miguel
$surname = Bacca
$dob = 04091992
$pob = Lr103
$marital status = single
.
.
.

%endwhois%
```

Other entries on the list, open to addition or modification as required, detailed family relationships, work experience, places lived, visited etc., languages understood (Spanish, archaic Spanish, American English mostly), as here we have just the beginnings, the basics of one Luis Miguel

Bacca, born on the 9th of April 1992, in Lr103 (as not yet mapped old style to new) – a bachelor. Zora's starriest students were nonplussed when all they had to do was learn a rudimentary mark-up language, with its percent and dollar strings, and by using one of her apps upload the list, where it embedded itself in the robot's artificial consciousness.

Tra-la.

33

She told her father she'd got those BoI people under control, a statement that set his scale of alarm somewhere off the green, for how did she think to resist these people? '*We* have all the power,' she said, not that Murillo could see it. She chose a quiet Sunday, and took the mazy walk from her end of the compound to his, when at four o'clock most officers were shuttered in their mess, playing a hand of poker, afloat on coffee, brandy and cigars. The men outside were in shirtsleeves, with a ball on an asphalt pitch, or clunking with improvised quoits (they were horseshoes). She took him to her second production line, a door off in a shadowy passage in a remote corner of her workplace, where in all stages of assembly she'd conjured replicas of both of them, jumbled and crated, and destined for addresses in Texas and California. 'Why on earth have you done this?' The professor's jaw dropped. Murillo looked pale.

'We will need decoys.'

'Decoys?' He examined the paperwork for each crate, authentic-looking forgeries, perhaps open to detection only by forensic means. 'How have you done this?'

'I have friends in low places.' One other forgery was a visa in the name of Hubert H. Gallenko, Jr., a man of Murillo's age, with Murillo's photograph. 'You are on leave next month,' Zora explained, and further supplied him with an air ticket to Miami, and a connecting flight to JFK. In his absence one of her replicas she'd put in his place – to date the most complete she had made of her father – to carry out his duties, answer questions, be a mouthpiece for the regime, and sit in his office with a careworn look. Murillo was always absorbed in the most complex technical problems.

Once he'd landed in New York there was an address in Wall Street he was to go to, by taxi, subway, or as he chose. There he would be met, by someone who would help.

'But—'

'No buts.'

'And what about you?'

'I will join you soon. Don't worry.'

His leave came round. He went home. He packed a case. 'Not too much luggage,' as Zora had said. 'You don't want to attract attention.' He set off under his Gallenko alias, I assume terrified, but at airport check-in aroused no suspicions and passed untroubled to the departure lounge. The flight was called, and he boarded. At Miami he was surprised when no posse of officials had gathered to detain then deport him. So on to his connecting flight, where a uniformed, hard-faced immigration officer drilled into his papers, but again frictionless progress on to the departure lounge. All day he had eaten nothing, but his stomach had settled and he took the chicken, the rice salad, and the cold tinned fruit served in-flight, and a daiquiri, for his digestion, in need of what help it could get. I don't know what arrangements he made for his final leg into Wall Street. I'd guess the airport shuttle into Manhattan, and from there a taxi. He found the address Zora had given him, and waited outside on the sidewalk, his battered, old-fashioned suitcase at his feet, and his raincoat draped over it – Gallenko bedraggled-looking. His liaison, Em, a familiar face, or rather I, a familiar face, did not find it hard to pick him out. On that flicker of recognition in his sad, sad eyes I shook his hand. 'Mr Gallenko. So glad you made it.' I carried his bag and took him off for debrief, where I told him my next assignment would shortly take me back to the UK, where my cover was as gossip columnist, outlook a deliciously biased, subtly distorting, hugely meretricious press, anchored in London with other infiltrating media. If he wished I could arrange asylum for him there. He looked bewildered. He didn't reply. 'You cannot go home,' I said, and when, to that, there was also no reply, I took it he'd choose to stay here, in hopes of reunion with his wife, Alejandra. Her curating, I knew, had projected her into New York's champagne high life, and he'd no longer understand her. 'There's no immediate hurry,' I said. 'For you, there are plenty of options career-wise.'

Zora's exit should have been as smooth, but wasn't. She

was too late for a temporary stop on the visa and other paperwork she'd got underway with her forger, an oldish man with a stoop and half-moon spectacles (I know him well), and instead asked for an adjustment – dates to be supplied. The reason? As a crack in the edifice and a shock that set her pulse on fire she was summoned by Forsiss himself, who must have penetrated to her schemes, with his spies out watching, listening, everywhere. He sent a car with the stoniest of cold, expressionless drivers, who without conversation drove her the hundreds of kilometres from Area 51 to Eutopium, or the presidential barracks there, the place under close guard and tight control. She expected the worst, but was dealt with hospitably, an honoured guest shown politely into Forsiss's office, that nerve centre of the new empire. She was served lemon tea and offered a selection of dried fruits, which she declined. Forsiss, formidable man of action, always in the lead, supplanting flag in hand and his feet on conquered ground, implacable in his masculinity and martial in his vigour – he was seated and withered and horribly frail. Zora perched on the edge of her chair, and waited, her gaze fixed across the desk (that box of cigars, that framed photographic portrait). His opening observation was erroneous in its assumption, Forsiss telling her how she had noted his recent absence from the political, public stage, though in fact she was too preoccupied with her own strategies to have paid him any heed. His removal from that bruising arena the General greatly regretted, as he knew how beloved of his people he was, an honest, peasant population who backed the reforms he had set in train, and in such a noble air, for above all it was the common people who had suffered the cost of national pauperism. Zora did not challenge that ideology, but listened to his proposal.

The General would not let his people down, come what may – and bizarrely that *come what may* was terminal decline. She'd be flattered to know he had chosen her as the only Utopian beyond his closed circle – men like Arango – to share in his revelation. For her and for those she represented he clung to the last modicum of magic and mystique our fairy tale of modern life makes of our leaders – it makes them unequivocally destined, put together transcendentally of wild unreachable stuff. It sets them apart. He told her the cancer he'd got would kill him, without revealing what kind of cancer it was. She would know only the end was soon. He coughed. He spluttered. He wiped a tear. 'I am sorry to hear it,' Zora said politely. She was less enthralled to know what, exactly, it had to do with her, though her president thought that was the one thing that must have been obvious. The F regime – his, Forsiss's regime – could not be allowed to falter. She would go back to Area 51, with whatever materials and information she needed, and using that amazing Murillo technology would construct a Forsiss lookalike, capable of sitting before a camera and microphone and delivering a script. His people would not know he had gone. She protested that what he was asking was huge in its technical challenges, with such short time available. He had every confidence, he said, and between them she and her father would not fail. 'I will go back and talk to him,' she said, with not the least irony in her tone, 'and see what he advises.'

'Thank you, Miss Murillo. You and your father have already signed the Official Secrets Act. In your case we have added a paragraph, and that you will also be asked to sign.'

'Of course.'

34

Another blow to the F regime was the fate of Manuel Arango. His evangelising zeal took him into bandit country, where – in one one-horse town after another – he mounted his soapbox and preached to the masses. In this case the 'masses' were a dribble of homey smallholders caught on the public square, pausing to listen only out of idle curiosity. Every little helps.

Arango was known for his punishing itineraries, and a lack of foresight in the planning of his pillow for the night, sometimes with no other option than camping out with his bedroll, under a bush, under a twinkle of coloured stars. Reports vary, but surveying them all (as I do conscientiously) I am clear of one thing. At dusk one evening Arango stumbled onto a trading outpost. There was minimal stabling and a makeshift bar – a plank between two barrels – where a toothless boniface served firewater to a staple of passing furriers. Most were known to him. Arango wasn't. Arango got himself to the head of the queue and ordered iced liquor, and asked – his tone fatigued and demanding – after food and lodgings. None of that was here. Nor were there recommendations. He showed his irritation in the shrug of his shoulders, and a hint of contempt. He downed a first shot in one. 'Another,' he said. He slid his glass across the plank. Next in line in a distinguished clientele was a big man with a beard and theriomorphic deities tattooed up his arms. He did not like Arango's girly looks, the locks of his shoulder-length hair, the bangles he wore on his wrists, the pointy point of his boots, or the Americano tightness of his jeans. He tried to pick a fight – his beard spongy with spittle – but Arango wasn't intimidated. In return he began to lecture him – for what was the F regime to an ignorant peasantry here? I will tell you. A loud cymbal crash that had reached precisely no one's ears.

Arango was left alone, and downed a second shot, a third, a fourth. His assailant amused himself outside. That big bearded man messed with his saddlebags. He secured his bedroll. He waited. I delve in my notes and see he is named variously as Bladimir, Leandro, Roel – all an evasion. Those names caught the imagination of someone in the Vespucci psychology faculty, who polished up an old theory suited to the moment. So now we have a Utopia unwilling to jettison its hero mythology, unable to shake off its strangulating grasp. As a ring round a cutthroat country, the mantic ouroboros is eternal in its circle, and combat is never ending. The shade Bladimir, the eidolon Leandro, the relic Roel, as natural magistrate of all-encompassing lawlessness, squared up to the reeling Arango as he stepped out into the dying light. Do not go gentle. Ambition aside, it shouldn't have been a contest, but Arango acquitted himself courageously, meeting blow with counter-blow. For a girl he packed a punch. The fight went beyond its predicted limit, two wrestlers squirming in the mud, till at last Bladimir called an end and drew his knife, and slit Arango's throat. I got the news and mixed reports when the country was in mourning, Arango's body having been shipped to the capital, cleaned up and shown off as messianic, and put on public display, in a composition reminiscent of Caravaggio's *Entombment*. Forsiss – the real Forsiss – led the nation's grief, but as a radio broadcast only, with TV adapted to it and cued with archive footage. The two men shaking hands. Forsiss brandishing a cigar. Arango hotting up the crowd. Banners. Street marches. A new dawn. A dead saint. After a lying-in and the laying of flowers, and queues kilometres long filing past the body, the body was put to rest, as was Forsiss's, only weeks later, but without that public awareness. Zora's prototype came on screen and delivered a simple message, the script pared to its essentials – how best to honour Arango's memory, with the F regime pressing on. And on.

It was a development I watched closely while coaching Murillo prior to his swearing of allegiance under the flag of his adoptive country. I worked hard in restraining him when in the short speech he wrote, in unbroken English, his first reference was to Gödel's Incompleteness Theorem, a fracture that with clever maths, logic and linguistics he applied to the Constitution. I also told him not to voice his observations on the country's schools, universities and its written and broadcast media – all of it a sameness to him – a discrete system of propagation in a stitching of political correctness and group identity. I struck out too his dismissal of a Congress bought by corporate interest. 'And you can't say either,' I told him, 'that the Federal Reserve ought to have been abolished.' He looked puzzled, but did as I told him, when only the day before I had shown how much I sympathised. 'Yes,' I said. It, the Fed, was a drain on individual liberty, on citizen vitality.

His greatest reluctance was in ditching his point-by-point deconstruction of the Second Amendment, doubting it as the right mechanism as counterweight to an oppressive presidency, or rule by a tyrant (something he'd personal, first-hand experience of), an interpretation open to multiple distortions, and at schoolyard level and up a disaster. Thankfully the whole thing passed off without a hitch, and in a few days I was able to introduce the professor to his new colleagues at MIT, where he was handed a cornucopia of funding and specialist facilities, and began building a team of handpicked personnel. Alejandra would have been proud. Zora, surprised.

I had some last things to do before my new assignment in London and Hoe, but couldn't have foreseen the delay, as I thought I had got Zora freely on her way as she followed her father out of Utopia, all tracks covered. Not so.

35

Zora's adopted identity in her flight across Cape Cold was of one Christine Whittaker, a young entrepreneurial housewife who had travelled south from South Dakota, with a line in franchise products – swimwear, cooking aids and other baubles – for recruitment into her beach and kitchen party biz. She'd notched up more than a century in a pyramid of like-minded people, a chain spreading its base under her sunburnt, sandalled feet. Zora knew nothing of her trade, but rehearsed her characteristics as she managed the Forsiss stand-in – any last teething troubles down to her to fix. Her free time was spent transiting between Eutopium and Area 51. In that latter location she left a replica of herself – her ZR001 – at work busily with her father, her RH001. ZR, RH: it's about to get more complicated. Her flight was an evening flight, but her connection wasn't to London – not immediately. Those stores she'd sent limbs and torsos to, with involuted circuitries, and heads and hair and flesh, in a deliberate mix-up, and Byzantine documentation with the crates the lot had been sent in – these were what fixed her tour through Texas and California. She hired cars, took trains, and boarded a criss-cross of internal flights. From all that detritus she assembled an extended ZR-RH range, replicants tilting the register as far as 009. Yes. She had read Philip K. Dick. I learned much later that someone very like Dr Murillo was spotted in Buenos Aires, another in Kiev, a third in Vienna etc. As for Zora, I have known her lookalikes turning up in Japan on a holiday ramble round that country, in the Czech Republic, on the Isle of Lewis, and at a therapy centre in southern Spain. There are more I do not list.

She might have got away with it but for a casual glance over a schedule of deportees by someone at the BoI. It appeared one Christine Whittaker, of the hated imperialists, had left the country twice, ten days apart. Further investigation showed she had gone out the first time under the digitised photograph of a freckled, sated, plain, horribly complacent, dark-haired bourgeois sickly in her smile, whose birthday was in April. Passport and visa details differed the second time only in one respect, that of the photo, which in a trawl through the BoI's census records was a match for Zora Murillo's – Zora a rare beauty, of reddish darkish hair and electric in her eyes. A call was put through to Area 51, the operative there insisting that no, Zora Murillo was here. Working. With her father. The case was escalated upwards, and got as far as a black-booted, black-haired, dark-suited, spectacled (tinted, yes), darkly sadistic doyen of BoI Interrogation, who had his valet drive him personally to Area 51, where he sauntered through security and burst in theatrically on Zora's work and office, demanding an explanation. She was laconic in her replies, oddly unperturbed (BoI Interrogation had a fearful reputation in a post-Morales, post-Silva, post-Arango world), and evasive in a non-committal way. That would not be tolerated. There were token protests, first from her father, then from Zora herself, when she was put in the car, and with her tormentor for company driven to BoI HQ. There she was placed in a cell, its only comforts a latrine, a hand basin, a hard cot with a single blanket, and a naked bulb that hung on a twisted wire. The wattage was low.

Her interview room was black cement walls, wooden chairs, and a steel-framed desk with stocks for the hands, where Zora's delicate, scented wrists were secured. Her examiner showed that the toes of his boots were steel, while the steel of his spectacle frames sparked off flints of gold, whether in sunshine or under artificial light. He spent ignorant hours getting nothing from her, despite the monstrous threats. Those threats became a reality when a taciturn Zora still did not comply. She was led to a second interrogation room, this one darker and more sinister, where a mannish-looking woman, pale complexioned and with the faintest of moustaches, supervised the removal of the subject's clothes – the last being the red lace of her underwear, ZR001 an idealised sylph – and cuffed her at the ankles and wrists to a low-lying iron-framed bed. There, for six hours, she was serially raped. It's the scene no clause in the sale of film rights will see downplayed as the climax, with professionals of that trade well versed in putrid stuff like this, the centrepiece, and deliciously disgusting as a fantasised reality. BoI specialists trained in information retrieval trotted in singly – a dwarf, a giant, a rake, an obese adolescent, a dirty old man, and so on – all with crotches in a bulge and pinned to their faces a salacious staged-up leer. The real Zora Murillo followed it on her laptop. In elapse time her ZR001 transmitted all that it recorded – sounds, pictures, the lot. No one on the ground understood. After tedious hours of elaborate, more penetrative, more violent thrusts, the doll remained impassive. No sound, no moan, nothing. So, gentlemen, what next?

'I'll give her one last shag.'

'Let's try ripping out her toenails.'

That eventuality wasn't arrived at, as now we return to the closed circle seated round the dummy president. There was general descent into panic once it was known the only person who fully understood its mechanism had been taken to the regime's most modernised theatre of torture. The helicopter now sent directly to that compound came with her rescuer, code name Zed, who got out of her everything that had happened. She was as calm, precise, and matter-of-fact as her torturers had found her. It dawned slowly, painfully, that Zora wasn't what she seemed. 'We must get you medical attention,' said Zed, using his head. She said it wasn't necessary, but the point was insisted on. Ergo she spent the following day at Forsiss's private clinic, somewhere in a leafy suburb of Eutopium, having her genitalia examined. Said the doc: 'Never seen anything like it.'

So to a further review of Utopia's deportation schedules, and the discovery that one Hubert H. Gallenko, Jr. – big in import-export – had been repatriated, and yet, to the contrary, was still here, in discussion with a scrum of town councillors – locality a dismal place down south – where both parties wrestled over his redundancy arrangements. He'd got warehousing, and a pre-Utopia workforce. With Forsiss having issued winding-up orders on foreign-owned concerns, Gallenko was negotiating severance and compensation, trying to argue the millions demanded were a sum he did not have. But let us not digress. The passport photo for the Gallenko who had left was not Gallenko's. You and I know it was Dr Murillo's, and the F regime soon knew that too. The small coterie in a rally round the nation's president – an emblem expressionless in its plasticity – demoted its motionless embodiment to a corner of the strategy room, where it sat in waxen pose with a hand raised and the butt of a cigar between two fingers – a ludicrous presence. What retaliation now could this, a select group of visionaries, envisage?

The first thing was to follow Murillo's movements, and find out where he was. That took time enough that when at last someone like him *had* been found – with a new identity – Zora was busy with more from her school of replicants. She stepped up production, off her conveyor, out to the world. The Murillo the regime hit on was seen leaving a frame house in Clarksville every morning, on the short drive to the laboratory where he had found new work and a new career in Tennessee. A car bomb was placed under the chassis, that action followed by a boom on next ignition, and then misleading claims. The F regime had placed a spy in the enemy camp, but what espionage he'd succeeded in had been discovered, and the FBI had dealt with our honoured hero callously – death by explosives. A

White House spokesperson came onto C-SPAN with the puzzling response that the F regime had made a bad case of mistaken identity, which was plausible only weeks later when a second Murillo turned up in Venezuela, the chief engineer on a highways project. When taken in secretly by the BoI he was tall, assured, untroubled in his movements, modest in his dress. He co-operated and showed no sign of trickery. Then after days of confinement he fell ill, with a plague-like disease, whose mark was fever and eruptions. He lay for twenty days with the pain of his sores. When those on his face improved his captors saw signs of recovery. But the fever worsened, and he'd no reserves of strength to resist. He couldn't speak or eat. On the thirty-first day he raised his hands in a gesture of farewell, and after that the body was hastily disposed of. There was no funeral as such, just a cremation, low-key and attended only by officials.

The exercise was deemed complete when, one lazy afternoon, the waxen likeness of the late President Forsiss whirred into life, when no one here had activated the app to make it do so, or told it what to say. Present were the elite in the small kitchen cabinet forging the future, faces blanked, jaws dropped, astonished. More so as Forsiss relit the stub of his cigar, took up a pen, and wrote: 'You will deposit 20,000,000 US dollars in this account. Here are the details.' In meticulous block script Forsiss set out Zora Murillo's offshore bank details. I can't say who it was with her, on vacation at Martha's Vineyard, Zora prone on her bed, and kicking off a slipper, and looking on through her laptop. It did no good to protest, she said – or rather Forsiss said it for her. She was sole possessor of the encrypted key – an innocent bit stream sent through the ether – that once transmitted signalled an end. 'My hand hovers on the button.'

'You will please explain that statement.'

It was simple. The F regime's fake president was a legacy product, retired on the spot, without the twenty mil.

36

I flew to London a few days before Zora, where I was due to begin my new cover as gossip writer. I met her at Paddington off the Heathrow Express, and took her for a pub lunch at a place I knew in Marylebone – oak panelling, solid furnishing, high moulded ceilings. 'Love it,' she said. She smiled and erupted into giggles when I told her I'd spent a morning at Madame Tussaud's, where I had lingered knowingly at the model of General Forsiss, while somewhere, in another latitude, off to my left, Benedict Cumberbatch was attracting most of the attention. (First job. I'd be interviewing him for a piece in the *Post*.) I told her about this out-of-the-way place called Hoe, where I had a riverside property. I had bought into the non-plastic-reuse ethos there. For my amusement, it was teeming with armchair Marxists, Jean-Paul's children of existentialism, *noms-de-guerre* politicos big in the Twittersphere, trashy stand-up poets, moody bloggers self-styled as fully versed in Keynesian economics. There were too the other usual bourgeoisie: solicitors, shop people, private and rental property agents, restaurateurs, Uncle Tom Cob et al. People came from all points on the globe for its proximity to the Tagore experiment, with courses offered in human-centred, eco-repro, fragile-earth awareness. There had been rickshaws powered by chip fat, an awful stain on the environment.

'I'll check it out,' she said.

Under her new identity – Zora Murillo now Zora Murillo (I hate those black redaction bars) – she went a step further than that. She bought the hotel in Yo, the Faun, but quickly tired of its county clientele and the routine of its afternoon teas. The Pleiades was more a Murillo challenge, though the news nexus (Mawdrie) and the petty commerce magnetising to it, were, in the end, an irritant. I thought she would go, but I knew not where, or when. Confirmation came on a crisp autumn morning when, with a gentle rap, she announced her presence in the porch as she stood at my cottage door. I should have noted this before (the door), with its blue panels, a black handle, a surrounding trellis in a twine of copper leaves. I deserve my rural peace.

I was almost ready, standing at the hall mirror – its silver framed in golden vines. I adjusted my neck gaiter, trying to get it to cover my scar. I put on my hat and opened up. She was radiant, and smiled, and had on a royal blue showerproof trench coat, the belt tied, not buckled, red denims, and soft leather slingback sandals, and was ready for a walk. We strolled along the path on that bit of it running parallel with the Dwar. Leaves fluttered down. Mist that had shrouded the valley began to dissolve under the reddish gold of a late September sun. We met Mawdrie coming the other way, who stopped and chatted politely but did not conceal the darting anguish in his eyes. Zora still didn't know what to make of him.

'He does not have the benefit of certain explanations,' I said, on a bend in the river.

'Explanations? He's a newsman. Historian. Where is his insight?'

He did not understand that 5,000-word essay she had sent him, with its emphasis on Styliane Psellus.

'How,' I said, 'is he supposed to infer Murillo private experience from that public Psellus drama? A lost child, political upheaval, a family in division.'

'He's at least supposed to be curious.'

Andalusia was her next destination. Planned to take her place was one in her ZR series. 'I might even program into it a fondness for Andrew Mawdrie.'

'Oh,' I said. 'Then where will we be?'

Our walk wound us further into the countryside, hills, a still river, Hoe a little toy construction out of sight and miles behind. As usual we stopped for lunch at the Huntsman's, where the terrace was screened and we sat outside. Bruno de Roon and friends had got there before us, and had pushed three tables together, and were partying over something – a birthday, an exam result, a new deal at the Parakeet. De Roon pushed the detritus left from his lunch – a strand of red onion – to the side of his plate. He drank heartily and regaled – not just those with him, but the whole echoing countryside – with that tale of his adventure on the moor, ending in his rescue by the owner of the Parakeet, Louella Ångström, the Lou I knew (and more than she knew I knew). I had trawled through her diary often, whenever I could, as weeks prior even to Madame Tussaud's she was under my surveillance, papers having come my way as to her liaisons with a man called Earl, who was caped, shadowy, and nationally a mystery.

But that's another story.

The Holly Scholarship

On a July day in 2018 my family was dealt a shattering blow, one we are not likely to recover from fully. That was when my daughter-in-law Holly, thrilled as we'd been to welcome her into the Cowlam clan, took her own life.

All who knew Holly are left to construct whatever personal memorial to her is most fitting to them. It may seem odd that mine is a story about a feisty young woman who has escaped the clutches of a military junta. I have two reasons for that choice. First, *Utopia* is the book I was working on at the time of Holly's death. But more important, twelve of its thirty-six chapters are set in the fictional locality of Hoe, a quaint English market town very like the one she and her childhood sweetheart, and now bereaved husband, Jack Cowlam, grew up in. She would have recognised many of Hoe's landmarks, and has shared much of its topology, though will have known none of its characters. The latter are purely inventions of mine.

Holly Cowlam dedicated her life to working with children with autism, and had the specific aim of bringing Applied Behaviour Analysis (ABA) into the mainstream. ABA is a therapy based on the scientific analysis of learning and behaviour. Its practitioners apply acute understanding of how behaviour functions, of how it is affected by environmental factors, and of how learning is actuated. The purpose of ABA is to augment behaviours that are helpful, and to diminish those that are either harmful or adversely affect learning.

For Holly, ABA had proved its efficacy with early intervention and individualised programmes for children living with autism. Her main area of professional activity was where autism spectrum disorder (ASD) had been diagnosed. Above all Holly was a committed advocate of ABA, strongly supporting its potential to create a secure, positive environment in the teaching of functional living and the nurturing of communication skills, so important to the children in her care.

Sadly Holly had been suffering from anxiety and depression, and on 9 July 2018 decided to end her life. There are many unanswered questions surrounding that decision. We will never know what depths of darkness she had entered, and by what feelings she was driven. What *is* certain is Holly never lost her passion for her work, having taken on the task of guiding all those who came under her supervision to the best of opportunities, through an education promoting maximum outcomes, no matter the challenge. She inspired others with passion and positivity, and brought out the best in those she worked with.

She leaves behind a husband in Jack Cowlam who wishes to honour her legacy in the form of an annual scholarship, the Holly Scholarship. Its *raison d'être* is to fulfil her goal of bringing ABA into the mainstream, and to provide yearly ABA scholarships for children living with autism. Proceeds from the sale of this book will go to that cause.

As a memorial *Utopia* cannot be complete without a word for the person most deeply affected by Holly's departure, her husband, my son Jack. The resilience and inner strength he has found in face of the most awful tragedy of his life – still a very young life – others, at times, have found hard to interpret. I say to them only they do not know the hours he and I have wept together, and will go on weeping, after his beloved wife Holly. Holly Cowlam, 13 February 1990–9 July 2018.

—*Peter Cowlam, July 2019*